The MAGNIFICENT
Mya Tibbs

THE WALL OF FAME GAME

Also by Crystal Allen

The Magnificent Mya Tibbs: Spirit Week Showdown
The Laura Line
How Lamar's Bad Prank Won a Bubba-Sized Trophy

The MAGNIFICENT Mya Tibbs

THE WALL OF FAME GAME

CRYSTAL ALLEN

Illustrations by Eda Kaban

BALZER + BRAY

An Imprint of HarperCollins*Publishers*

Balzer + Bray is an imprint of HarperCollins Publishers.

The Magnificent Mya Tibbs: The Wall of Fame Game
Text copyright © 2017 by Crystal Allen
Illustrations copyright © 2017 by Eda Kaban
For information address HarperCollins Children's Books,
a division of HarperCollins Publishers,
195 Broadway, New York, NY 10007.

www.harpercollinschildrens.com

ISBN 978-0-06-234236-2 (trade bdg.)

Typography by Carla Weise
16 17 18 19 20   CG/LSCH   10 9 8 7 6 5 4 3 2 1
❖
First Edition

To Heather Renz, Kay Reidy,
and all dedicated teachers and
librarians around the world.

Thank you for making a difference.

Chapter One

I push my cowgirl hat down on my head until it feels just right and then straighten my new outfit. I don't need anyone to tell me how boo-yang good I look in my new Annie Oakley skirt and vest. Mom made one for me and one for herself. Ever since kindergarten, we've worn matching outfits to Open House, and tonight, we're going to be the best-lookin' cowgirls on the planet! And as a bonus, I've got a folder full of A+ papers just sitting on my desk, waiting to make Mom holler "Yee-haw!"

But when I get downstairs, Mom is still in her robe, sitting on the sofa with Dad. I think you have to sit a lot when you have a little one in your belly. Mom's nine months pregnant with my baby sister, Macey, and she's always sitting, which proves my point. She said this October is the hottest one she remembers here in Bluebonnet. Maybe so, but if Mom doesn't hurry, we're going to be late to Open House.

I smile and twirl slowly so she can see how awesome I look. "I love this outfit and can't wait to see yours. You better get dressed. It's almost time to leave." Her face has a lot of sad in it. "I'm sorry, Mya. I won't be going to Open House tonight."

I stare at Mom, waiting for her to say something like "Just kidding!" or "Gotcha!" But she doesn't.

There is nothing worse than a bad surprise, and I just got one.

"But, Mom, you always go to Open House," I say.

"It's still hot outside, Macey's been kicking all day, and my stomach's sore. I hope you understand," she says.

I'm trying, but right now, the only thing I understand is that I made all of those good grades for nothing. At every Open House, Mom gives me super-duper hugs that make me feel good from my boots to my braids. That's not going to happen tonight.

My brother shuffles over and stands beside

me. His real name is Micah, but I call him Nugget because his skin is brown and his head is shaped like a chicken tender. He's wearing a T-shirt that reads *Does the Name Pavlov Ring a Bell?* It doesn't to me, but Nugget laughed out loud when he saw it at the children's science store.

"Sorry you're going to miss Open House, Mom," says Nugget.

She nods at him. "Me too."

Dad lowers his face to Mom's stomach and talks to it. "Macey? It's Daddy. What are you doing in there? Are you playing baseball?"

I clear my throat, even though there's nothing stuck in it. "Huh-*hmmmm!* So Dad, are you taking us to Open House? I don't want to be late."

He checks his watch. "Is it that time already? Let's go!"

Mom waves to me. "You're not upset with me, are you, Mya?"

I shuffle over and hug her with both arms. As Mom keeps rubbing her stomach, I'm thinking maybe it's good she's not coming with us. If Macey's kicking because she's trying to find the exit door out of Mom's belly, I don't want her poppin' out during Open House.

So tonight, it will just be Dad, Nugget, and me.

3

That's not as fun as having Mom with us. Dad gives fist bumps, and my As are super-duper-hug As, not fist-bump As.

On our way to Open House, the heels of my pretty pink boots go *ka-clunk, ka-clunk* when they touch the sidewalk. They're supposed to, because that's how real cowgirl boots sound. We walk and talk about Open House until Nugget changes the subject.

"Dad, did you see the pitching line-up for game one of the World Series? The Yankees are throwing Wicked Willie Combs."

Dad puts his arm around Nugget's shoulder. "The Cardinals are going to have a hard time hitting Wicked Willie's curveball."

I keep walking, hoping this conversation doesn't last, because I don't know much about baseball.

Nugget kicks a rock off the sidewalk. "I've been studying his pitches. Now I can tell what Willie's going to throw before the announcer calls it. It's all in his arm motion," he says.

Dad chuckles and shakes his head. "Son, you're a baseball genius! I've never met anyone who can pick up baseball facts like you do."

I tug on Dad's shirt sleeve. "Excuse me, but we're on our way to Open House, not the ballpark."

Dad's eyes widen as he smiles. "Yes, ma'am!"

As we get closer, cars and trucks line the street in front of Young Elementary School. Little kids run in the grass as groups of grown-ups talk and laugh under the streetlights.

"Hey, Nugget, wait up!"

It's Fish Leatherwood and his dad. Fish is my brother's best friend. His real name is Homer because his dad loves baseball, but Fish looks more like a boy than a home run. It's his big blue eyes that got him the nickname Fish. I can only look at them for so long, and then I get dizzy. Tonight he's wearing a T-shirt that reads *Either You Like Bacon or You're Wrong.*

As our dads shake hands and talk, Fish gives Nugget a fist bump and then turns my way. "Hiya, Mya Papaya!"

I love when he calls me Mya Papaya. It's not a good western name like Annie Oakley, but I still like it. "Thanks, Fish. I like bacon," I say, and point to his shirt.

"Me too," he says.

I add some giddy-up to my walk when I see Principal Winky at the front door. He's dressed in a blue suit and white shirt. Those are our school colors! He waves and gives us a big Texas-size smile.

"Here comes my favorite plate of Fish Nuggets and a Texas cowgirl! Yee-haw! It's Open House, and we're going to have a wonderful evening at Y.E.S. Yes, yes, yes! Please take a program off the table on your way inside. Classrooms will open in thirty minutes. Until then, there are lots of things to enjoy, like refreshments and face painting in the cafeteria, picture taking for a good cause near the library, and of course, catching up with your neighbors. Have a wonderful time, yes, yes, yes!"

"Let's go get some punch," says Dad.

"We'll see y'all in Fish and Nugget's Open House," says Mr. Leatherwood.

Fish nudges me. "I bet Mrs. Davis talks about the Wall of Fame Game tonight. That's what she did last year when Nugget and I were in her class. Don't forget to sign up for it."

The smile slides off my face. "I'm not signing up for the Wall of Fame Game. Annie Oakley's movie marathon starts next week. Mom and I already have plans to watch it. I just need to get my folder and take it home so Mom can see it."

"Oh, okay, that sounds like fun," says Fish. "See you later, Mya Papaya."

I guess Fish doesn't check the *TV Guide*, or else he'd know that Annie Oakley's movie marathon starts on Monday, the same day the Wall of Fame Game begins, and there's no way I can do both. If I signed up for the Wall of Fame Game, I'd have to study from the time I got home from school until I went to bed. Good gravy. Why would anybody want to do that?

I'm not making my brain do any extra remembering, and that's what the Wall of Fame Game makes everybody do. The truth is, this Wall of Fame Game isn't really a game at all. It makes kids study a bunch of boring facts when we could be having boot-scootin', loud-hootin' fun.

I know a dirty rotten trap when I see one. And I'm not falling for it.

Chapter Two

This has to be a record-breaking crowd for Open House! It's so loud in the cafeteria that at first I have to cover my ears. Voices echo off the walls as people stand around talking and holding cups filled with punch and little snack plates. If we were this noisy during lunch, Mrs. Davis would stand on the stage, hold up two fingers, grab the microphone, and count to five—that means zip your lip. But I don't think that's going to happen tonight.

There are two refreshment tables against the back wall. One has fancy bowls filled with red and blue punch. The other has cookies, cakes, and three big veggie trays with ranch dressing. On the other side of the cafeteria, there's a long line of kids waiting to get their faces painted. As I *ka-clunk* over to the veggies, I spot my best friend, Connie, and her little brother, Clayton, standing next to their mom.

I run to them as if we haven't seen each other in weeks, even though I just saw Connie in school a few hours ago. "Hi, Mrs. Tate. Hi, Clayton. Hi, Connie."

Both Mrs. Tate and Clayton hug me. Connie and I grab little plates and fill them with carrot and celery sticks and a glob of ranch dressing, and then shuffle back to the hall.

"It's kind of creepy being in school at night, isn't it? Where's your mom?" asks Connie.

This feels like the perfect time to tell a taradiddle. That's cowgirl talk for a story. I put my plate down on the table with flyers about Open House, hold both edges of my vest, and look as serious as I can.

"Mom's surfing the Nile, Amazon, and Mississippi, trying to set a record as the only pregnant woman to catch a wave on the three longest rivers in the world."

Connie laughs and rolls her eyes. "You and those taradiddles. And I don't think you surf rivers. You surf oceans."

I pick up my plate and sweep a carrot stick through the puddle of ranch dressing. "Well, it's true what I said about the rivers. They're the longest ones."

Connie and I both chomp down on the veggies. Her head tilts as she chews.

"Geez, Mya, how do you remember that stuff?"

I smile. "Every taradiddle a cowgirl tells has some facts in it!"

Connie nudges me with her elbow. "Speaking of remembering stuff, are you signing up for the Wall of Fame Game? You should. I bet you'd make the wall. The way you hold on to facts, it would be easy as cake. We could sign up together!"

I flip my wrist at her. "No way. There's an Annie Oakley marathon starting on Monday. It's kind of a big deal for Mom and me. We wear our cowgirl hats, eat popcorn, chew beef jerky, and drink lots of root beer. Dad even brings Buttercup into the house. When Annie chases the bad guys, Dad puts me on Buttercup and I pretend I'm riding with Annie to catch them!"

Buttercup is our mechanical bull. Everybody

from bullriding beginners to cow-ropin' profes-
sionals likes to climb on his back for a spin. I'm not
afraid to ride him, but only on level one.

"I saw a commercial for the marathon on the
western channel. I bet you and your mom have a
bunch of fun," says Connie.

I grab a celery stick from my plate. "After that,
Mom and I have to get ready for the chili cook-off
next week. Cowgirls first, chili second. I can't wait!
Look out, Annie Oakley, 'cause here I come! Yee-
haw!"

There's lots of noise coming from the hall by the
library, so we make our way to the front, and find
Starr and Skye Falling smiling and greeting people. On the other side of them is Naomi Jackson, my
old best friend, and her parents, looking proud and
happy.

Skye holds up her camera. "We're helping Naomi.
For a small donation, you can get your picture taken
with her dressed up as Junior Miss Lone Star."

Naomi's wearing a white pageant gown, a blue
sash across her shoulder that reads *Junior Miss
Lone Star*, and of course, her shiny tiara.

"She's charging money to get a picture taken
with her?" asks Connie.

I shake my head. "I can't believe it."

Skye nods. "All the money goes to the homeless shelter. You want to get a picture taken with her?"

Connie frowns. So do I. Naomi is the one who gave both of us our terrible nicknames—Mya Tibbs Fibs and Mean Connie Tate.

It's been three weeks since I lassoed Naomi in the hall during Spirit Week. I remember like it was yesterday. Connie and I had just become friends, while Naomi and I dropped from BFFs to worst enemies. So when I had spotted Naomi leading a stampede of students toward Connie's art room, I'd thought she was going to trash it. I had to do something.

So I did.

Right there in front of my classmates, I lassoed her. In four seconds flat! I got in trouble for it, but I also set a new roping record.

I know she hasn't forgotten. I haven't, because it was one of the best roping days of my life. But I know she's going to try and get me back for that.

I take off my right boot, turn it upside down, and shake it over the donation bucket. Two quarters fall out.

"That's all I have. I don't want a picture with her, but I do want to help the homeless," I say.

Nugget and Fish race by on the way to their

classroom. Dad and Mr. Leatherwood wave at Naomi and her parents, and they wave back. That's when I notice Naomi watching me. She rolls her eyes. I roll mine back. Dad puts his hand on my shoulder.

"We're heading to Nugget's classroom, Mya. Meet us there in two minutes."

"Okay, Dad," I say.

Connie's mom waves as she leaves the cafeteria, holding Clayton's hand. He's got balloons painted on his face.

"Your little brother is so cute. I hope Macey makes people smile as much as he does," I say.

Connie sticks her tongue out at him. He laughs, and so does she. "Anyway, Mya, about the Wall of Fame Game—I'm definitely signing up. If I make it, I'll be the first Tate on the wall. Both my parents tried, but they missed two questions on the last day. I think they'd be really proud of me if I made it. Have you ever read all the names on the wall?"

I shake my head. "Every time I try, I lose my place and have to start over. There's so many names up there."

"I know! It looks like a thousand!" Connie walks toward our homeroom. "I bet your two minutes are up. You better get to Nugget's class before your dad comes looking for you. I'll see you in Mrs. Davis's room. We are going to have the best Open House."

I head in the opposite direction, toward the fifth-grade hall. "It's going to be a yippee-ki-yay kind of Open House, Connie! I can't wait!"

Chapter Three

Imake it to Nugget's classroom and stand next to Dad and my brother. The teacher, Mr. Booker, makes Nugget sound like the smartest kid in the universe. Dad grins as Mr. Booker hands him a flyer about Whiz Kid Camp. It's a special science and math place for geniuses. Mr. Booker didn't actually say "geniuses" when he gave Dad the flyer, but I bet he was thinking it. Dad takes the flyer and winks at my brother. Nugget looks down at his shoes, but I can still see the grin on his face.

Mr. Leatherwood has a flyer, too. He shows it to Dad. "Mr. Booker is coaching Bluebonnet's Little

League team this fall. Fish and I have been waiting for him to be old enough to play in this league! Is Nugget going to play?"

Five more dads gather around Mr. Leatherwood. They have baseball flyers, too. Dad shakes hands with all of them before answering. "I didn't know anything about it. Nugget definitely knows baseball, but I'm not sure he's interested in playing."

It seems like every dad around us slides his eyeballs down to glare at my brother. It's quiet for a moment, and I feel like it's time to go, but Dad doesn't move.

"Not interested! Aw come on, Tibbs! I'm sure he's got some of your baseball blood running through his veins," says Mr. Leatherwood. "I remember playing ball with you from Little League all the way up to high school. You were the only guy in Bluebonnet who got a baseball scholarship!"

The other dads nod and tell stories about how good Dad was at baseball. Mr. Leatherwood nudges my brother. "I'm sure you want to play, don't you, Nugget?"

Dad moves Nugget behind him and faces the other dads. "I've got a feeling my boy's more interested in that Whiz Kid Camp."

Solo Grubb, the coolest fifth grader in our school,

joins the group. He's wearing sunglasses, even though it's dark out. While the dads are talking, he whispers, just loud enough for me and my brother to hear.

"Yo, Nugget, doesn't your dad want you to try out for the team?"

Now Nugget's whole face frowns. "Mind your own business, Solo!"

Solo holds up both hands. "It was just a question. Chill out."

I finish the last of my veggie sticks, throw my plate in the trash, and then tug Dad's sleeve. "I think we should get going to my class now."

"Me too," says Dad. He shakes the other dads' hands again. "I'll see you guys around. Have fun at the ballpark. Come visit the store when you have a chance."

I hope Mrs. Davis gives Dad a flyer for me. Maybe there's a cowgirl camp with line dancing, and calf-roping lessons and a trail ride. I'm good at calf roping and two-stepping.

On our way to my class, Nugget's face is wrinkled with mad, and he's talking to himself.

I lean toward him. "What's wrong?"

"Leave me alone, Mya," he says.

"But you're going to ruin my Open House with

that face! I didn't ruin your Open House, did I? So don't go ruining mine!"

"You didn't ruin it, but somebody else did."

I *ka-clunk* closer to him since we're almost at my classroom. I know he's talking about Solo. So I give him an earful. "Listen, Nugget, don't let Solo change your happy mood."

His face is still angry, so I add a bit more. "He's just being a jerk. He's probably worried that if you try out, you'll show him up. You know more about baseball than . . . than whoever invented it."

Nugget doesn't answer, but I keep walking with him, hoping he'll smile, but he doesn't. Soon Mrs. Davis greets me with a pat on the shoulder and shakes Dad's hand.

"Mya, I love your outfit! You look like you should be in the Cowgirl Hall of Fame!"

I grab the edges of my vest and grin. "Thanks, Mrs. Davis."

She pats Nugget on the shoulder, too. "And here's one of my star students from last year."

"Hey" is all he says before walking into my classroom. It's one thing to be mad and not want to talk about it, but it's a whole other thing to act grumpy at my favorite teacher. I give him a stink eye that I hope he can smell.

Mrs. Davis tells Dad that I'm an excellent student and my grades prove how hard I try. I keep listening as I watch my brother sit down with his bottom lip poked out. My face warms, because if he was going to be upset, he should have done that in his own classroom, not mine.

All my classmates step out into the hall so the parents can talk to Mrs. Davis. I join them.

On normal school days, standing out here means you got kicked out of class, but not tonight. Mary Francis talks first.

"Connie, are you signing up for the Wall of Fame Game?"

She nods. "Definitely."

Lisa pulls a tissue from her purse as she sniffles. Her nose leaks more than my bathroom faucet. "I don't know if I can remember all those facts. Mrs. Davis hands out the questions right before we go home. That means I'll have to study all night before *and* after dinner. That doesn't sound like ahh . . . ahh . . . *achoooooooooooo!*"

We turn away from her and close our eyes.

"Sorry, everybody," she says.

Soon Skye, Starr, and Naomi join us. Naomi stands next to Kenyan, and the twins come over by me. Sometimes it's hard to believe Naomi wins so many beauty pageants with that bad attitude she's got. All the judges see is her skin that's the color of buttermilk pancakes and her wavy hair, how it seems to blow off her shoulders even when there's no wind. I think it's her green eyes that make the judges pick her. What those judges don't know is that Naomi is also green on the inside, and it's a stinky, dusty, moldy green.

She glares at me. "Hey, Mya Tibbs Fibs. Cute outfit, but don't you ever wear anything besides those ugly pink cowgirl boots?"

I don't answer her for three good reasons: she called me that terrible nickname, and my boots are not ugly—but the biggest reason is that Naomi's fake, phony, and full of baloney.

She rolls her eyes. "I bet you don't even own a regular pair of shoes. I have eight different pairs, all different colors. When you have to create a port-folio for beauty pageants and modeling agencies, you can't wear the same things for every picture. Anyway, are you signing up for the Wall of Fame Game? I'm not sure how big a cowgirl's brain is, but if it's not big enough to keep a promise, it's defi-nitely not big enough to remember all those facts."

Just last month, Naomi and I were best friends—until I accidentally broke a promise to her. We were supposed to be Spirit Week partners, but I pulled Connie's name out of the partner-picking hat, and Connie wouldn't trade partners so I could be with Naomi. Naomi was friend-ending mad at me. I tried to say I was sorry, but instead she started calling me Mya Tibbs Fibs. Now we're enemies for eternity times infinity.

Why does Naomi care if I sign up for the Wall of Fame Game? Why does anybody care? First it was Fish. Then Connie. Now Naomi. I'm already sick of hearing about it, and I'll be so glad when it's over.

Chapter Four

Naomi steps closer to me. "I asked you a question, Mya Tibbs Fibs. Are you signing up for the Wall of Fame Game? Not that it matters—everybody knows you're not as smart as your brother."

All eyes move from Naomi to me. Heat rises from my boots, through my legs, up my spine, and into my brain. I don't want to get in trouble again, especially since Dad's right there inside my classroom. I want Open House to be awesome, and it won't be if I stay here arguing with Naomi.

Connie whispers to me. "She's just trying to get you in trouble."

I nod. "I'm going back in to make sure Dad found my folder. You can—"

Naomi interrupts me. "Hey, Mya Tibbs Fibs, I just remembered something. I bet you're not playing the Wall of Fame Game because there's an Annie Oakley movie marathon next week. I thought about you when I saw the commercial. I just can't believe anyone would choose a dumb western over getting your name on the wall, but what can you expect from someone who watches baby stuff like cowgirl movies and dresses as if she's in the Wild Wild West."

That's it. I show her my fist. "Take that back, you tiara-wearing turkey! You think you're so smart!"

As I'm stepping toward Naomi, Connie gets a handful of my vest. "Stop, Mya. No name-calling. Just because she does it doesn't mean you have to."

"I'm five hundred times smarter than you!" says Naomi, stepping into the middle of the circle.

I pull away from Connie and join Naomi with my hands on my hips. "I bet you get all of your Wall of Fame Game answers ping-pong, ding-dong, double-X wrong!"

It's dead-people quiet around the circle except for Lisa's sniffles. Naomi crosses her arms. An evil grin spreads across her face.

"Are you playing in the Wall of Fame Game, or are you chicken? Everybody in here knows that celebrities like me are way smarter than cowgirls, and I'm going to prove it."

Good gravy in the navy. She just insulted the entire cowgirl nation right in front of my face! My eyes half close as all eighty of my teeth—or however many I have—clamp for battle.

"You can't prove that, because it's not true," I say.

She walks as she talks. "It's easy to prove. At the end of the Wall of Fame Game, whichever of us has answered the most questions correctly will be the smartest. If we tie, nobody wins. But if one of us misses more questions than the other, the loser has to bow to the winner and admit she's not as smart. And all that bowing and admitting has to be done in the cave, in front of the whole class."

Connie whispers in my ear. "Don't take that bet, Mya."

Everybody's looking at me. Naomi just called me out like the bad guys called out Annie Oakley, back in the Wild West, for a duel in the middle of the street.

I whisper back to my best friend. "I don't have a choice."

Naomi puts her hands on her hips. "So are you in or not?"

I stand tall and speak for every member of the cowgirl nation, dead or alive.

"I'm in! And Mrs. Davis should start a Wall of *Lame* for trash talkers like you!"

Connie taps my shoulder. "Mya, let's get out of here before you get in trouble."

Naomi puts her finger on her chin and stares at the ceiling. "Wall of Lame. Yeah, let's add that to the bet. The loser bows to the winner, plus has to wear a lame T-shirt. Why don't you have your new BFF, Mean Connie Tate, make us one, since she's so artsy-smartsy?"

My face must still have anger on it when I turn to Connie. "Make it extra lame."

Connie tries to pull me away. "Mya, I don't think this is a good idea."

I yank my arm from her grip. "Sometimes you have to shut people up! Think about all the ugly things she's said about us. This is your chance to get her back, too, Connie. You can make the lamest shirt ever, and she'll have to wear it!"

I'm expecting Connie to look pumped up, but she doesn't. Instead she just shrugs.

"Fine. I'll make the T-shirt."

Naomi looks at me. "So does this mean we have a deal?"

I cross my arms over my chest. "Whatever makes your socks stay up."

Naomi gets closer to me. "Good. And no takebacks."

My classmates shake their heads and shuffle back into our classroom. The longer I stand there, the more I realize I just got suckered. Naomi's last words bang around inside my empty head. *And no takebacks*. That means I can't say I was just kidding, or I didn't really mean it. Or flat out say I made a mistake.

I grab two of my braids and pull down on them as I close my eyes. What was I thinking? Saying yes to the Wall of Fame Game also means saying no to Mom and me watching the Annie Oakley marathon. I rub the side of my head because I'm sure it's going to start hurting soon. Connie's still with me. Everybody else is inside the classroom.

"Let's go in, Mya. There's nothing you can do about it now. You heard Naomi. No takebacks."

She's right. Firecrackers! I take a deep breath and follow her into the classroom.

My classmates stare at me when I walk in. I spot Nugget still sitting in the same chair with his lip poked out. I don't even care about that anymore. I've got bigger problems.

Our teacher raises her hands in the air. "Welcome, everyone. Please take a seat. My name is Mrs. Davis, and I'm the fourth-grade teacher. I'd like to speak with you about the Wall of Fame Game. First let me give you a little background. Many years ago, a teacher by the name of Mrs. Heather Renz created what we now call the Wall of Fame Game, an exciting question-and-answer game of facts."

I look over my shoulder. Naomi's looking at me. I frown and then turn back to Mrs. Davis as she continues to talk.

"Every student who masters the Wall of Fame Game gets their name added to the wall in the back of this classroom. The word FAME is an acronym meaning 'For All My Efforts.' The names of the students who make the Wall of Fame will never be painted over. Now we're edging close to seven hundred names on the wall, including congressmen, farmers, judges, store owners, and more. For some students, their entire family is on the wall."

I think I'm going to be sick. I lean back in my chair, hoping to make myself feel better.

Mrs. Davis continues. "Two weeks ago, I handed out study sheets with various subjects and categories.

Every day next week, each student will get three Wall of Fame Game questions taken directly from the study sheets. On Monday, each question will require one answer. On Tuesday, each question will require two answers. On Wednesday, three; Thursday, four . . . and the big finale will be on Friday when each question will require five answers!"

There's lots of mumbling and whispering as everybody figures out what I already know. That's way too much studying. Mrs. Davis continues.

"At the end of the week, if a student gets all of the answers right, or misses only one question, his or her name will become part of the Wall of Fame forever!"

As everyone claps, I scratch my arm and neck even though they're not itching. I turn around and stare at the Wall of Fame. It seems bigger than it ever did before.

Dad leans toward me. "Are you okay? You don't look so well."

"I'm fine," I say.

Mrs. Davis continues. "For those of you who've never had a close look at the Wall of Fame, I'd like to give you that opportunity right now. If any of my students would like to sign up for this year's Game, the sign-up sheet is on my desk."

I spot Naomi Jackson walking toward the sign-up sheet. She stands in front of it, staring at me as she picks up the pen and then points it in my direction. I can feel my classmates' eyes bouncing from Naomi to me. Dad puts his hand on my shoulder.

"Your mom wanted me to tell you that she doesn't want you signing up for the Wall of Fame Game just because your brother did. I totally agree with her, understand?"

I nod my head, but it's too late for that kind of talk. I *ka-clunk* to Mrs. Davis' desk, take the pen, sign my name, and then drop the pen on top of the sign-up sheet.

"There, I did it. You're going down, Naomi," I say.

She grins at me. "We'll see about that, Mya Tibbs Fibs."

My face gets crooked. "Yes we will, Naomi, fake, phoney, and full of baloney."

I see Dad looking my way, so I straighten all the crooked in my face and smile as I make my way back to him.

"I signed up for the Wall of Fame Game."

He holds out his fist, and I bump it. "Well, okay. Good luck, Mya."

We walk to the wall and stare at all the names. "For all your efforts, Mya. That's what this wall is all about," he says.

I just nod and stare because I'm not signing up for the Wall of Fame Game for any other reason than to beat the stew out of Naomi Jackson.

Chapter Five

O pen House is over, and so is my life. I just gave up the best western marathon ever, to do schoolwork. If I could get my boot up high enough, I'd kick myself in the back of my skirt.

It's so quiet on the way home that I feel like I'm walking with two strangers. The *ka-clunk* of my boots is the only sound. Nugget's staring at the sidewalk with his hands in his pockets, and Dad's not talking at all.

I'm walking as fast as I can to get home so I can show Mom this folder of A+ papers and then start studying. How in the world am I going to become a genius over the weekend? There're over fifty different questions I have to memorize. Fifty!

When Mrs. Davis gave us the study sheets, I stuffed them in my boot because I had no plans to sign up for the Wall of Fame Game. I don't even know where those sheets are right now. I'm lucky Mrs. Davis had extra study sheets on her desk. I grabbed a set on my way out.

I can't let Mom or Dad know my real reason for signing up for the Wall of Fame Game, because I'm sure I'll get in trouble. They'll try to tell me that my reason isn't very honorable, and winning a bet is the only thing I'll have For All My Efforts.

But right now, that's all I want.

Dad unlocks the front door and turns on a light. It's just as quiet in here as it was walking home. Mom's asleep on the couch. Dad touches her shoulder. "Honey?"

Mom wakes up and rubs her belly. "I'm okay; just tired. Macey finally stopped kicking about ten minutes ago, and I'm cold."

Dad helps her off the sofa. "Come on, you need to lie down."

I step to the other side of Mom. "I brought my folder home for you to see."

Mom smiles. "I'll look at it later, Mya."

"Right now your mom needs rest," says Dad.

I nod like I understand, but I don't. Mom didn't go with us because it was too hot outside, and Macey *was* kicking. Now she can't even take two minutes to look at my folder because she's cold, and Macey *stopped* kicking. This has been the worst Open House ever. And I haven't even told Mom the bad news about our Annie Oakley marathon. If Buttercup had feelings, I'm sure he'd be sad, too.

I climb the steps to my room and open the door. My life-size posters of Annie Oakley and Cowgirl Claire stare back at me. They're both wearing jewelry I made, because I taped earrings and necklaces to the posters.

"It's not my fault, Miss Oakley. I got suckered. You want to see my folder? Nobody else does."

I wonder if this is the beginning of how my life is going to be when Macey gets here. Mom will be busy with the baby, and I'll be stuck doing things all by myself.

Knock, knock.

Nugget's standing at my door with his hands still in his pockets. He steps inside my room. "I need to talk."

He paces, and I let him because I'm in a horrible

mood anyway. When he turns to me, his face is full of mad.

"Dad thinks I'm a loser."

I plop on my bed. "Dad doesn't think you're a loser."

"Then why didn't he ask me if I wanted to try out for baseball? I'll tell you why. Because Solo was right. Dad thinks I stink at sports. I remember, back before kindergarten, being in the backyard with him, tossing a baseball. I only remember two days of Dad trying to show me how to bat and catch. I guess he didn't think I was going to be any good. He didn't even bother to finish teaching me how to play."

I wrinkle my face to match his. "I don't understand what you're talking about, Nugget."

He sits on the edge of my bed. "It's as if Dad doesn't even want to *try* and help me be better at baseball. Mr. Leatherwood and Fish go to the batting cages and play catch almost every day. Dad and I used to play ball in the backyard, and then we just stopped. Bam. Nothin'. Now he's all excited about Macey being a ballplayer. Did you hear him say that when Mom said Macey was kicking?"

I nod.

He gets up and paces again. "Dad's waiting on

Macey to play baseball because he doesn't think I can. I must be the biggest loser ever if Dad's picking my unborn baby sister to play baseball over me. We almost missed Open House because he was so busy trying to talk to her through Mom's belly." I read in *Science* magazine that infants hear voices while still in the womb. I bet Dad was telling Macey a bunch of batting tips that he never told me."

I shake my head. "Don't blame Macey."

He snaps at me. "I'm not!" His head lowers as he sighs. "Sorry. Didn't mean to yell at you."

"It's okay. I don't know anything about that science stuff, but I was really looking forward to watching the Annie Oakley marathon with Mom, and signing up for the chili cook-off. She loves Annie Oakley as much as I do. Now I have to do the Wall of Fame Game instead."

I feel kind of itchy about telling Nugget the truth. It doesn't matter why I signed up, does it? I'm doing the Wall of Fame Game. No one has to know my reasons. But that's not my problem right now. I go stand next to my brother.

"Do you think Mom and Dad will be too busy for us when Macey comes? You don't think Mom will back out on the chili cook-off, do you? That's all we've got left to do together."

My brother just stares at the carpet, and I'm wondering if he even heard what I said. That's when I stare at the carpet with him and tell him what's really hurting me.

"Mom didn't even look at my folder. It's full of A+ papers, Nugget. Do you know how hard I worked to get those As? Mom made me feel like it doesn't matter. Who's going to care about my good papers after Macey gets here?"

Suddenly he puts his arm around me without saying a word. I know what he's trying to tell me. I lean on his shoulder.

"Thanks, Nugget. I'll always care about the things you do, too."

He nods and walks to my door. "I'm going to bed."

As soon as he leaves, I get my stuffed animals out of the bottom drawer of my dresser and set them up in different places on the carpet. With a quick swoop of my hand, I grab my rodeo rope that's hanging on a knob sticking out of my wall.

Before I get started, I put on a pair of earrings and two bracelets I made. One day I'm going to be the best calf-roping jewelry maker who ever lived in Bluebonnet.

I make a big lasso and throw it at the black bull.
Missed.

As I pull the rope back, I think about all the studying I have to do for the next seven days. That's bad. But then I think about the chili cook-off. It will be just Mom and me. I'll have her all to myself. That's good!

I *ka-clunk* over to my computer desk, take a seat, and read over the study sheets. Look at all these questions—history, science, geography, and even sports. My knee's jumping under the table, and I can't make it stop. I already know the answers to some of these, but a lot of them are hard.

Mrs. Davis gave us the websites where we can find the answers. She even made answer lines on the study sheets for us to fill in. My answer lines are blank. I bet I'm the only person in my class with blank answer lines. That's because everybody else started filling in their answers two weeks ago, when Mrs. Davis first handed out the study sheets. It wouldn't surprise me one bit if Naomi has all of the questions memorized.

I wonder what Naomi is doing right now. Is she studying? Is someone helping her memorize the answers to all these questions? That's what I need— a study partner. I'll ask Connie.

I pick up my rope, twirl it in the air, and look for my next victim.

The longhorn cow.

I keep my eye on him as I swirl that rope in the air. *Come on. I can do this.* I let the rope go and watch it soar through the air toward the longhorn.

Got 'im!

I flip that longhorn, tie up his legs, and hold up my hands to prove I'm finished. My bedroom is quiet. I look around at all the other stuffed animals on the floor. They're in a big, wide circle, just like my classmates were tonight when Naomi challenged me. I stare at the longhorn with the rope wrapped around him. I bet all he wanted to do was stay in the drawer with his friends. Now look at him, tied up in something he can't get out of.

He reminds me of me.

I untie the longhorn, put away my stuffed animals and my rodeo rope, and then put on my pajamas. As I lie in bed, thinking about Mom, Macey, the Wall of Fame Game, and Naomi, I get scared. I need extra time for Mom and the chili cook-off. But if I'm going to beat Naomi Jackson, it'll take everything I've got, and even that may not be enough.

Chapter Six

I had a rough time sleeping last night. I kept thinking about what happened at Open House between Naomi and me. But it's Friday morning, and that means the weekend is almost here.

I'll have two whole days to study and figure out how I'm going to beat Naomi before the Wall of Fame Game starts on Monday. The last thing I do before I leave my room is stuff both feet inside my pink boots without sitting down. That's how real cowgirls put on their kickers.

Downstairs in the kitchen, Mom waddles and wobbles from the bright red stove to the counter.

Her feet *swish-swish* across the floor in the cow-girl slippers Nugget and I bought her. She used to wear real cowgirl boots just like me, but it's hard to *ka-clunk* around when you're about to download a baby.

On the counter is a peanut butter-and-onion sandwich. I smell it before I see it, and I wish Mom craved something more normal, like ice cream. But then she'd probably put onions on top instead of a cherry! As I watch her stir whatever she's making in that pot, I get excited knowing that soon we'll be making chili together for the cook-off next Saturday.

I give her a big hug. "Good morning, Mom. How's Macey?"

Mom hugs me back and rubs her belly. "She's up playing baseball again."

I look around for Nugget. I'm so glad he didn't hear that. I put my hand on Mom's. "There's something I need to tell you about the Annie Oakley marathon."

She keeps slowly stirring whatever is in that pot. A grin wider than the Amazon River spreads across her face. "Your dad told me you signed up for the Wall of Fame Game! Oh, Mya, this is so exciting! Let me know if you need help, okay? And don't worry about the Annie Oakley marathon—we'll catch the next one."

Mom gives me one of her super-duper hugs. She's holding me so close my face is smashed against her belly. I bet Macey is eyeballing me through Mom's belly button, pointing and laughing. For some reason, I thought Mom would be upset, like she and I got ripped off somehow, or the Wall of Fame Game stole our time together. I thought she might cry, but she doesn't seem bothered at all about missing the movie marathon. Is Mom too busy for me already?

Nugget shuffles into the kitchen. There's a copy of the *Bluebonnet Tribune* under his arm. He reads it every morning, almost as if the front page said, "Dear Nugget."

"Greetings and salutations, my lady," he says, bowing to Mom.

She curtsies back. "Greetings and salutations, Sir Nugget. Here's your oatmeal."

He takes his bowl. "Congratulations on your last doctor's appointment today," he says.

"Thank you! To celebrate, I'm going to the grocery store afterward to get everything for the chili cook-off," she says.

A spark of hope rises in me. "We're going to win again this year, right, Mom?"

Nugget holds Mom's hand in the air. "Two-year defending Bluebonnet Chili Cook-Off champion, going for the trifecta!"

Dad strolls into the kitchen, gives Mom a smoochie, and then rubs her belly. "How's that ball-player?"

Nugget puts his bowl on the table, turns to Dad, and smiles until he realizes he's talking about Macey, not him. On his way to the breakfast table, Dad tickles me until I scream, then tries to wrestle Nugget for the newspaper. Instead of keeping the paper away from dad, Nugget just hands it to him.

"Here. I'm finished with it anyway."

Dad's smile goes away. "Are you okay this morning?"

"I'm great," says Nugget, but his face doesn't match his words.

Dad gives Mom a look and then shrugs. After he blesses the food, Dad lifts his coffee cup. "I need help at the store tomorrow with a large order of supplies that came in. Plus, I'm expecting some of Macey's furniture that was on back order to be delivered to the store. I've got to put that crib together, and the dresser, too."

He rubs his eyes, yawns, and takes a sip of coffee. "Anyway, the supplies have to be stacked and shelved. Both of you can count on working at the store all morning, okay? Mya, I know you're going to get Monday's Wall of Fame Game questions today. Bring them with you. Tomorrow is going to be a long day, but I'm going to make time to quiz you on my break."

Dad owns Tibbs Farm and Ranch Store. It's filled with everything farmers and ranchers need, plus a whole lot of other stuff, like sports equipment, pet food, clothes, and shoes.

I sit up and lean over the table. "Can I ride Buttercup at the store?"

"Not tomorrow. I'm going to be really busy for the next few weeks."

"Okay," I say, and pick up my spoon.

I can feel Nugget looking at me and then at Dad before finishing his oatmeal.

"Let's go, Mya," he says.

We're halfway to Young Elementary when my stomach feels like butterflies are flapping their wings and flying inside. I should never have taken that bet with Naomi. Maybe I can still get out of it. I tap my brother on the shoulder.

"I feel bad about skipping out on the Annie Oakley marathon. I know Mom didn't show it, but I could tell she was disappointed. I could change my mind and—"

He interrupts me. "Listen, Mya, I shouldn't be telling you this, but the Wall of Fame Game is more important than you think it is. Don't play around, okay? Do your best. Today is practice for Monday. Make it count."

"I know how important it is, Nugget. Mrs. Davis already said—"

He interrupts me again. "No. It's something more than that, but I can't tell you."

Holy moly, Nugget's got a secret! I move my backpack around so that I can unzip a side pouch. I reach inside and pull out an old sour apple Jolly Rancher. The candy's a little melted, and stuck to the wrapper, but I can tell it's still good.

"You can have this if you tell me the secret. It's your favorite flavor, too."

I can tell he's getting weak because he swallows twice. Then he shakes his head.

"No, I can't."

"I'll throw in my dessert at lunch."

Nugget rolls his eyes. "It's fruit cocktail day. You can't make deals with fruit cocktail."

I shove my things back into the pouch of my backpack and zip it. "Fine! Don't tell me! And don't worry about me playing around with the Wall of Fame Game. I've got my reasons for making it. And I bet my reasons are way more important than yours."

At least I know Nugget's got a secret about the Wall of Fame Game. He has no idea that I have one too! I grin, feeling smarter than my brother on my way to Mrs. Davis's room.

One of the best things about my class is the Cubby Cave. We just call it the cave because fourth graders wouldn't be caught dead using words like cubby. We have cabinets, not cubbies. They look like lockers, only more awesome.

To get to the cave, you have to walk exactly eleven steps past Mrs. Davis's desk and turn left. There's a big tunnel opening with rainbow colors painted above it that reads "The Cubby Cave."

Mrs. Davis calls the cave an adjoining accommodation, whatever that means. It's more like a superhero's secret hideout because you can't see it from the hallway. That makes it boo-yang cool! Each of us has our own cabinet to hang up our coats and backpacks and to store supplies. But the best part is we get to hang out in there before the bell rings and after school.

Today it's super loud inside the cave. Everybody seems happy, not nervous.

And then Connie walks in.

All talking stops. All moving stops. She's carrying

something on a hanger, covered up with a black plastic bag. I feel as if I'm going to throw up. Everybody knows what it is. Kenyan points at the bag. "I bet that's the lame T-shirt Connie said she'd make for Mya and Naomi's bet."

The crowd moves closer to Connie, and Naomi squeezes through until she's right in front of my best friend. My heart's beating like there's three of them in my chest instead of one. Connie lifts the plastic from the hanger and holds the T-shirt up high for all to see. Naomi gasps. I feel dizzy. A few kids cover their mouths in horror.

Connie parades around the cave, holding the T-shirt high in the air so everyone can see. It's a white T-shirt with Flowerhead Babies all over it, from the number one lamest show on television, *The Baby Garden*. There's Tuliphead babies sucking bottles, Rosehead babies taking a nap in a garden, Sunflowerhead babies crying, and they're all in diapers with dirt on their faces! At the top of the shirt, it reads *I Am a Flowerhead Baby*.

Good gravy in the navy.

Connie talks loud enough for everyone in the cave to hear. "Whoever loses the bet has to put on this T-shirt as soon as the bell rings after school on Friday. And they have to wear it all the way home."

She then turns to Naomi and me. "Hold up your right hands and swear!"

I raise my right hand. "Swear."

"Definitely, swear," says Naomi, with her right hand raised.

Connie hangs the T-shirt in her cabinet and continues. "At lunch, I'm taking the T-shirt to my art room to lock it up. I'll bring it back on Friday after lunch."

Naomi grins at me. "You're going to look great in that shirt when I beat you."

I frown at her. "We'll see who's wearing that shirt next Friday."

Lisa sniffles and wipes her nose as she walks between Naomi and me. "Don't you realize what you've done? Whoever loses doesn't just lose the bet. One of you is going to lose your reputation and be the biggest joke in Bluebonnet. Like maybe forever."

The expression on Naomi's face changes to terrified. I wonder if my face is showing the same frightened look. Thanks to Lisa, Naomi and I know that we didn't think this bet thing through before agreeing. It's bigger than we imagined.

One of us is going to lose everything.

Chapter Seven

That T-shirt Connie made is the worst T-shirt in the history of T-shirts. Last night, when I agreed to the Wall of Fame Game bet with Naomi, it was all about who's the smartest. Now that the loser has to wear this lame shirt, it's about our reputations, too.

Connie puts her hand on my shoulder. "Don't be mad at me, Mya."

"I'm not. Naomi's the one who should be mad. She's going to have to wear it," I say.

Skye and Starr walk over to me, holding hands. Skye plays with one of my braids.

"That shirt is lame, lame, lame," says Skye.

"Super lame," says Starr.

"I hope you're ready for the Wall of Fame Game," says Skye.

"You better be ready," says Starr.

I nod, even though I'm not even close to being ready. "Don't worry. I got this."

"Anything fun happening this weekend?" asks Starr.

"We're looking for something fun," says Skye.

I keep my eyes on Naomi as she walks toward the classroom. "Nugget and I are working at the store in the morning if you want to help."

Skye raises her hand. "I do!"

Starr raises hers, too. "Me, too! Mom and Dad are going to be testing their new extended-lens telescope for up-close planet observation. Snore."

"A total snore," says Skye.

"I'll come help, too," says Connie. "It shouldn't take us all weekend to study, should it?"

I giggle. "I hope not. We better get to our desks so we're not marked late."

Soon the morning bell rings, and Mrs. Davis grabs her attendance book. I push a pencil off my desk—but gently, so it doesn't roll too far away. As I bend over to pick it up, I turn my head to face the back of the room. I stay bent over, low to the ground, looking sideways at the Wall of Fame. From down here near the carpet, it looks like thousands and thousands of names spread across that wall, even though I know there's not that many.

I slowly glide my eyes to the far right of the wall, to the last row. I start at the top and come down four names. There it is, the name I've looked at a hundred times.

Micah "Nugget" Tibbs.

He thinks he has a big secret about why I need to make the Wall of Fame. Now that I've seen the T-shirt, my secret just got a million times bigger than his. I can never tell Nugget about the bet. He hates Flowerhead Babies as much as I do. If he knew there was a chance that I'd have to wear a T-shirt covered in them, he'd be so mad. I grab my pencil and sit up.

After the announcements, Mrs. Davis talks. "Today is practice day for the Wall of Fame Game. Let's begin. Raise your hand if you know the answer."

Naomi and I exchange evil eyes. She rolls hers, I roll mine. She shakes her head, and I do the same. But now I have a chance to show her just how smart cowgirls are.

I exercise my hand and fingers to make sure they're loose and ready to be the first one in the air. The muscles in my arm jump like a race-car driver revving his motor. *Vroom! Vroom!*

Mrs. Davis walks in front of the class. "How many members are there in the United States House of Representatives?"

My hand shoots up. I'm halfway out of my seat, leaning over the front of my desk when I realize . . . I don't know.

Mrs. Davis strolls to my desk. "Mya?"

I close my eyes, lower my head, and mumble, "Firecrackers."

"Excuse me? What did you say?" asks Mrs. Davis.

Michael turns to face me. "She said 'firecrackers.'"

I'd really like to tell Michael he's the biggest tattletale on the planet, but Mrs. Davis is standing at my desk, waiting on an answer that I don't have. "I . . . uh . . . just give me a minute to think, okay?"

"You won't have much time during the Wall of Fame Game, Mya," she says.

This can't be happening. I've got to come up with an answer, but I don't have one.

"Would you repeat the question, please?" I ask.

She nods. "How many members are in the U.S.

House of Representatives?"

It doesn't sound any easier the second time I hear it, so I look my teacher right in the face and tell her a taradiddle. "At night in Washington, DC, when the streetlights come on, I'm sure *all* those representatives have to be in the house." I look around the classroom. "Does anybody else have to be in when the streetlights come on? I do."

"I do," says Mary Francis.

"I do," says Kenyan.

Everyone's nodding, including Naomi.

"That's not the answer I was looking for, Mya," says Mrs. Davis.

"But it was a good taradiddle," says Skye.

"A very good taradiddle," says Starr.

Lisa waves her hand like she's drowning and needs a lifeguard. Mrs. Davis calls her name, and she answers. "There are exactly four hundred and thirty-five members of the House of Representatives, and one hundred in the Sena—ah . . . ah . . ."

All heads lower, and we cover our necks just like in a tornado drill.

"Achoooooooooo!"

I bet Lisa's sneezes cause cattle stampedes and dust storms. If Mrs. Davis had asked me how many times Lisa blows her nose in class every day, instead of that House of Representatives question, I could have told her.

"Sorry," says Lisa as we all look around for sneeze damage.

"You may want to keep a tissue in your hand, Lisa."

She sniffles. "Yes, ma'am."

Mrs. Davis grabs a stack of papers from her desk. "All right, class, these are Monday's Wall of Fame Game questions. You have all weekend to study. Every day next week, those of you participating in the Wall of Fame Game will get a handout with three questions. The handouts will be different, so each student will have his or her own questions to answer. I'll hand them out before the after-school bell rings."

Good gravy. I didn't know that. How can I study with Connie if our questions are different?

Mrs. Davis keeps talking. "After the announcements, I'll call students starting with the row closest to the door. When you hear your name, come join me at the front of the room. We will walk together to the back of the Cubby Cave, the traditional place where Wall of Fame Game questions are asked and answered."

Kenyan raises his hand. "How will you know when our time is up?"

"I have an egg timer. When the timer dings, the challenge is over. All questions must be answered, in their entirety, before the timer goes off, or it will be considered a missed question. A perfect score is fifteen. In order to make the Wall of Fame, you must get at least fourteen questions right. Remember, I count questions, not answers."

Mrs. Davis puts the stack of papers back on her desk, holds up both hands, and smiles. "That's it! If you need more explanation, please see me at lunch or recess."

If that House of Representatives had been a real question, I would have been hogtied and helpless, and only one question away from elimination. I need to put my thinking cap on. I've got to tighten my belt, and . . . whatever else I need to do to get through this.

The day drags, but at two thirty, Mrs. Davis hands out our Wall of Fame Game questions.

WALL OF FAME GAME QUESTIONS FOR MYA TIBBS:

MONDAY

1. Name a famous scientist.

2. Name a Native American tribe.
3. How many members are there in the House of Representatives and Senate combined?

Questions one and two are simple. I love math, and sometimes I love science, so I'll pick Albert Einstein for my scientist. I'm not sure about a Native American tribe, but thanks to Lisa, I already know the answer to number three! For a quick moment, I smile and relax, but seconds later, I feel sick. This is just the beginning. It's going to get harder. A lot harder.

Mom says, "If you want to cook a frog, you put him in cold water first, so he'll be good and comfortable. Wait awhile, and then turn the fire on low under the pot. Slowly keep turning up the heat. By the time that frog realizes things are getting hot, it'll be too late."

I feel like I'm sitting in a pot of cold water right now because these questions are easy-breezy. But I know Mrs. Davis is going to turn up the heat. The only way I won't end up being a dead frog is to figure out how to study, and what to study, so I can stay in the game without getting cooked.

Chapter Eight

I'm so glad it's Friday, and school is over for the week. At home, I let my backpack slide down my arms and onto the sofa. Mom's sitting with her legs propped on pillows. I sit next to her. Since the weekend is here, I've got a little extra time to relax before I have to study Monday's Wall of Fame Game questions and answers. Mom smiles, and for a moment, I think back to all the Friday afternoons when we'd get our nails done at Mani-Pedi by Betty. And every Wednesday, Mom and I would sit in front of the television with cheese popcorn and lemonade, watching Wednesday's Wild Wild Western movie together.

But we haven't gone to see Mani-Pedi Betty in months. And Mom falls asleep so early now that I watch the westerns by myself.

"Hey, Mom. Did you go to your appointment? What did the doctor say?"

She touches my hand. "He said I have to stay off my feet. I can only stand for three hours a day. That means the rest of the time, I'm supposed to keep my legs propped on pillows. Look at my swollen ankles. And he said I couldn't eat any more peanut butter-and-onion sandwiches."

Ya-hoo! No more stinky sandwiches! If I could climb on top of the roof, I would dance until Dad came and made me get down. But Mom's face is so sad. I hold her hand.

"Back in the old west, ankles used to swell up all over the ranch. Those cowgirls figured out the peanut butter they ate was sliding all the way down to their ankles and staying there. That's not swelling, that's peanut butter!"

Mom laughs, and so do I. "Mya, you and your taradiddles. But part of that is right. The salt from the peanut butter is what's causing the swelling."

I nod. "You'll be better soon. Did you go sign up for the chili cook-off today?"

The Annual Chili Cook-off is a big event in Bluebonnet. There are always a bunch of chili makers, but only one award. The winner gets an apron that says *I Make the Best Chili in Bluebonnet*. Mom's already won two aprons, and she even lets me wear one! It's not easy making first-place chili, but working with Mom in the kitchen is so much fun. But the sad is still all over her face.

"Mom?"

She shakes her head. "Oh, Mya, that's what I'm trying to tell you. We won't be able to enter the chili cook-off this year."

This can't be happening. I exhale without inhaling first. Two bad surprises in two days. Both from Mom. That has to be a record. Maybe I misunderstood her, so I flat out ask again.

"Are we or are we not doing the chili cook-off?"

Mom shakes her head, and stares at her ankles. "Making chili takes a lot of time and patience. You can't rush it, Mya. There's stirring on the stove, walking back and forth to the pantry to add this spice or that spice . . . and the doctor won't let me do it. I have to think about getting Macey's room ready.

I haven't even put away the presents from the two baby showers! These ankles couldn't have swollen up at a worse time. I'm so sorry, Mya."

Sometimes I wish I was Annie Oakley, so I could jump on my horse and ride as fast as I can, and as far away as my horse will take me. But I'm not her. All I can do is lean my head on Mom's shoulder. We sit in silence because there's just nothing to say. My brain makes a movie out of the memories of cooking with her during the last two chili cook-offs. I hold her hand again as I remember how much fun we had, how proud we were when we won, and how awesome she looked in that best-chili apron.

I hate seeing it as a memory, and not something I'm going to be doing soon. Mom and I should be adding another cook-off to this brain movie.

"So what now? You didn't come to Open House last night. We're not watching Annie Oakley because of the Wall of Fame Game. Now you're telling me the doctor took away the chili cook-off. This is like . . . I'm so sad right now, Mom."

"Me, too, Mya," she says as she rubs her thumb across the back of my hand.

"Everybody is going to be upset that we're not in the cook-off this year," I say.

Mom sighs. "Not everybody. Some people will be very happy about it."

I sit up. "No way."

Mom's chili is lick-the-bowl good. And when she's making it, the whole house smells just like I imagine food in the old Western movies would smell. I can almost hear Mom telling me what she does to get that special flavor. *"I take my time. No shortcuts. Everything has to be done with love and patience, Mya. You can't change those things. I put the meats, spices, and sauce in a pot together so they can introduce themselves to each other on a low fire. Then I'll put a top on the pot, and let all those different ingredients become family. That's what the letters in chili stand for: Cooked How I Love It."*

Mom lifts her feet off the pillows and stands. "Come walk me to my room. I'm going to lie down for an hour."

I take her hand, and we walk together as she talks to me. "The cook-off is very competitive, and we've won the last two years. Some people will be very excited for the chance to take my first-place apron this year. It's okay. You have the Wall of Fame Game you have to study for, and I have to take care of myself and Macey. But I'm sure going to miss competing this year."

I help her lie down. "Something could change. Your ankles could unswell! It ain't over till it's over, right? That's what you always say."

"Well, the deadline to sign up for the cook-off is tomorrow, and I don't think my ankles are going to be better by then," Mom mumbles as her eyes close.

I'm so sick of bad surprises. Right now, I feel like a balloon that someone stuck a pin in.

The chili cook-off is important to me. It's important to Mom! We do this together every year. I guess I should say . . . we *did* it every year, before this one.

I close her door and tiptoe into the living room to get my backpack. The doorbell rings, and I see Connie standing outside. I open the door, and then put a finger to my lips. "Shhh. Mom's taking a nap. Let's go upstairs."

I tell Connie what happened. She looks as sad as I feel. I turn on my radio and listen to a country-western song about a brokenhearted girl. That's the perfect song for me right now. Connie shuffles around my room.

"Hey, look, it's not like it's the end of the world, Mya. You can always enter the chili cook-off again next year. And your mom has to be careful. I mean, she's got to think about your little sister. One day you'll be happy that she chose to back out of the competition."

My shoulders lower, and my body feels so heavy. "Yeah, you're right. Mom's and Macey's health come first. But I'm still sad about missing the cook-off."

Connie grabs my rodeo rope off the wall. "Anyway, let's talk about the Wall of Fame Game. Have you figured out how you're going to study for the questions?"

"The only plan I have is to beat that trash-talking Naomi Jackson."

Connie tries to twirl my rope in the air, but she can't.

I giggle as I watch her. "I was hoping you would be my study buddy."

Now her feet are tangled in the rope, and she has to sit on the floor to untangle herself.

"We won't have the same questions."

I keep giggling. "I know. But we can still help each other memorize the answers."

She throws the rope at me and grins. "Actually, that's a great idea. And we can quiz each other, too, because at some point, the questions you have one day may be the questions I have on a different day."

"That's exactly what I was thinking," I say.

Connie grins. "Perfect. Hey, where's Nugget?"

"He's in his room, sorting his baseball cards for the thousandth time."

Connie sits on my bed. "I didn't know Nugget was into baseball."

"He's a baseball genius! I've heard him tell Dad things that even Dad didn't know about the game! But he's not very happy right now."

Connie shakes her head. "Oh. Is he going to be okay?"

I shrug. "He said when he was little, Dad stopped teaching him how to play baseball because Dad thinks he's a loser. Is that, like, the dumbest thing you've ever heard?"

Connie makes a funny face. "Uh . . . yeah."

I'm walking and talking now. "And then Dad said something about Macey playing baseball in Mom's belly. So now Nugget thinks Dad is looking forward to playing baseball with Macey instead of him, and he's trying to figure out how to spend time with Dad before Macey downloads, because after she's born, Dad might not have time for him."

Jambalaya.

That's exactly how I feel about Mom. I stare out the window, not really looking at anything. "You know, don't think I'm weird, but I totally understand what Nugget's doing. Now that the Annie Oakley marathon is off, and the chili cook-off is canceled, Mom and I don't have any plans. Nugget's right. Once Macey gets here, we'll be invisible."

Chapter Nine

I love Saturdays, but I don't like this one. Usually I'm doing things with Mom on the weekends, or at least planning for something fun that's going to happen next week. But the last two things on my calendar to do with Mom got kicked to the curb, flat-out canceled. Now my calendar is as empty as my piggy bank.

I sit on the edge of my bed and wonder if this is what my Saturdays will be like when Macey gets here. Am I going to have to work at the store every weekend? I don't want to empty boxes and stock shelves *every* Saturday morning.

But today, Dad needs me.

This morning, I set my alarm a half hour early so I can study my Wall of Fame Game questions. I wonder if Naomi's up. She probably is, and I bet she's already memorized her answers to Monday's questions. I won't let her beat me. That's why I'm up, too. Dad's going to ask me for the answers while we're at the store, so I better know them. I already chose Albert Einstein for my famous scientist. I'll never forget Lisa's answer to the House of Representatives and Senate question. The only one I need to memorize is a Native American tribe. I'm thinking it would be fun to choose Native Americans with a Texas connection.

I turn on my computer and Google Texas Native Americans. Holy moly, look at all the information from this website about the story of Texas! It says the Caddo tribe was here over a thousand years ago, according to archeologists! Whoa. And they actually came up with the name Taysha, which means friend, but the Spanish people translated it to Tejas, which means Texas! I've never heard of the Caddo tribe. Their history is really interesting. I'm going to pick them. I wonder what I'd find out about Albert Einstein if I Googled his name.

I'm so caught up in reading about Caddo history

and my favorite scientist that I lose track of time. I take a quick shower and put on my work uniform. It's time to take off my Wall of Fame Game thinking cap and put on my Tibbs's Farm and Ranch Store hat.

Our store has been in the family for years, and I know my parents are so proud to own it. My great-great-grandfather started Tibbs's Farm and Ranch Store a long time ago. Then he passed it down to his son, and it kept getting passed down like a pair of boots, until it got to us.

I stare in the mirror to make sure I look nice and neat. The bright red T-shirt and cap make me feel like a professional. Maybe I should practice acting like one. I smile at the mirror and hold out my hand as if I'm shaking a customer's hand.

"Howdy! Whatcha lookin' for?" Ew. I sound double dorky. "Hi, welcome to Tibbs's Farm and Ranch Store. Are you just browsing, or can I help you find something?"

Nailed it! Time to go.

It's not long before Dad pulls into a parking space at Tibbs's Farm and Ranch. Fish and his dad stand near the store door. Connie and the twins are there, too. Nugget rolls down the window.

"Greetings and salutations, Mr. Leatherwood!

What's up, Fish? Wow, it's a party!"

I nod at my friends, then whisper their way. "Watch this."

With confidence, I *ka-clunk* over to Mr. Leatherwood and hold out my hand for him to shake. "Good morning, Mr. Leatherwood. Are you just browsing today, or can I find you help something? I mean, can I browse you find nothing?"

Skye crosses her arms and shakes her head. "Horrible sentence structure."

Starr does the same. "Just horrible."

Connie giggles. "You need to work on your customer service skills, Mya."

Mr. Leatherwood chuckles and shakes hands with Dad. "I need four big bags of weed killer and two bags of fertilizer for my yard. We're getting it in shape for baseball season."

"Sounds good. Come on in." As soon as Dad unlocks the door and opens it, a cowbell rattles.

Clankity-clankity-clank.

That's how we know when customers come in. Dad and Mr. Leatherwood walk side by side toward the lawn supplies. Fish, Nugget, and Connie walk behind them, and I *ka-clunk* with the twins. We're all quiet as Mr. Leatherwood talks.

"Baseball tryouts are tomorrow. Our boys are

finally old enough to play real baseball, not that T-ball stuff."

Dad tosses two big bags of fertilizer to Mr. Leatherwood, a bag of weed killer to Nugget, and another one to Fish. Then he picks up two more bags of weed killer as they head to the front counter.

"Mya, come ring these up for us," says Dad.

Holy moly! It's been a month since Dad let me use the cash register. Last time I used it, I gave a customer an extra ten dollars. Not because I couldn't count, but because I overheard them say they were hungry but had used their money on the supplies they'd just bought at our store. I felt great about sending them to the Burger Bar for lunch. Dad did not.

Connie and the twins rush behind the counter to watch me. I feel like a rock star holding the scanner and running it across the bar code on the weed killer bags. The prices show up on the register. Nugget and Fish walk toward the door.

"We'll put these on the back of your truck, Mr. Leatherwood," says Nugget.

"Tibbs, you were the best ballplayer we had back in the day. Sure would like to see if some of that rubbed off on your boy," says Mr. Leatherwood.

Dad puts both bags of weed killer on the counter.

"I just don't think my boy's the baseball-playing type. He's more of a team owner than a player."

"OMG, Nugget was right," says Connie in a whisper.

I'm scared to turn around. Maybe Nugget didn't hear that. I scan a bag of fertilizer and look his way. His back's to me, but he and Fish are staring at each other. Fish opens the door. Nugget follows him outside and down the sidewalk.

Clankity-clankity-clank.

I give Mr. Leatherwood the bill. He gives me cash, and I make sure he gets the right amount of change. "Thanks, and come again," I say.

"Thank you, Mya," he says with a smile before turning to Dad. "Should I put the weed killer down first, or the fertilizer?"

While Dad and Mr. Leatherwood talk, Fish and Nugget come back in. Connie, the twins, and I follow them to the back of the store. Instead of putting on his work gloves, Nugget rips open supply box after supply box with his bare hands. Some boxes have overalls in them. Others have camping gear and big cooking pots. We're all scared to say anything to him. He looks up at Fish.

"At least you and your dad have baseball. Seems like he's always doing stuff with you."

Fish shakes his head. "Only during baseball season. One of the first things he ever bought me was a glove. I was two! Sometimes I wonder if I'd even play baseball if Pop didn't love it so much."

Nugget stops opening boxes. "Are you serious? I thought you loved playing."

Fish shrugs. "I do, but it's not my number one reason for trying out. This is the only time of the year that Mom and I get to see Pop, because he works so much overtime at the factory. But no overtime during baseball season. After every practice last year, he took me out to get a hot dog or a burger, just him and me. We didn't talk about his job. We talked baseball. But when the season's over, he goes back to working overtime. Baseball season is all I've got with Pop. That's my top reason for playing."

Mr. Leatherwood calls from the front of the store. "Hey, Fish! Let's go, slugger! How about we stop at the Burger Bar and get some breakfast? We can have some pancakes and a protein smoothie. Sound good?"

Fish gives us a long look. "He loves baseball more than anything."

Just as Fish is about to leave, Nugget grabs his jersey. "What time are tryouts?"

"One o'clock."

We all glance at the clock on the wall. It's ten thirty.

Nugget wipes sweat from his face. "See you there."

I rush over to my brother. "You can't be serious."

He rips open another box. "Come to the ballpark at one o'clock. You'll see how serious I am."

Holy moly. Nugget stinks at sports. And the only thing he'll hit with the bat is himself. I really need to be at home studying, making sure I don't miss any of Monday's Wall of Fame Game questions. I'm sure Naomi's working on her answers.

Beating that tiara-wearing turkey is number one on my brain, but I love my brother. I've got to be there for him at the ballpark, just in case he needs me.

Chapter Ten

I can tell by the way Nugget's ripping open boxes and yanking out supplies that he's madder than a rodeo bull. My friends and I stay away from him. The twins walk side by side as they take shirts, pants, and overalls out of boxes and fold them before placing the stacks on our display table. Connie grabs camping gear and stocks it in the camping aisle.

Clankity-clankity-clank.

A woman with short, twisty curls walks in wearing jeans, a white blouse, and western boots as red as her lipstick. It's Mrs. Frazier from our church. Dad walks over to her.

"How you doin', Mrs. Frazier?"

She walks down the aisle. "Fine. Do you have any of those heavy metal kettles like your wife used last year in the chili cook-off?"

Dad nods. "I just got one in, and it's on sale for seventy dollars."

"Oh, perfect! How's Monica, and the baby?" she asks.

I smile at her. It's so nice of her to ask about Mom and Macey.

Dad's face wrinkles a bit. "Monica's got swollen ankles. The doctor shut her down."

I'm sad all over again, thinking about my conversation with Mom last night.

"What about the chili cook-off? Tomorrow's the last day to sign up," says Mrs. Frazier.

Dad grabs the heavy metal kettle. "I'm afraid she's out of the running this year."

A smile bigger than Texas spreads across Mrs. Frazier's face. Connie stops stocking. The twins stop folding. Nugget watches her, too. When she sees us glaring, her face changes from glad to sad. "Oh, I'm so sorry to hear that. Tell Monica I'll be thinking about her."

Dad brings her the kettle. "Do you need me to carry this somewhere for you?"

"Yes. Would you please put that in my car? It's unlocked."

"Sure," says Dad. "Mya, ring up Mrs. Frazier's kettle for me, please."

When the cowbell rattles, Mrs. Frazier rushes to the front. I silently signal the twins to follow her on the other side of the store. Connie stands near Buttercup and pretends she's dusting his head. I *ka-clunk* up to the front like I own the place.

"Will that be all?"

"Yes," she says.

Mrs. Frazier glances at the door and then lifts her neck up like a turkey to look toward the back before pulling out her cell and punching in a number. Soon she turns her back to me and moves farther away from the counter. She's whispering, so I step closer and listen.

"Hey, I've got good news! Monica Tibbs isn't going to be in the chili cook-off this year. Yeah, she's got swollen feet or something. I'm at the Tibbses' store, picking up one of those kettles she used in the contest last year, and I just found out! Isn't that awesome news? What? No, I'm not going by to see her. I've got chili to make. It's time for a new champ, and this is my year. Just thought you'd want to know. We'll talk more later."

She stuffs her phone back in her purse. "Okay, what's the cost?"

I thump numbers on the cash register without even knowing the bar code of the kettle, and then I press the total button.

"That will be six hundred and fifty-four dollars."

Her eyes get as big as the cash register. "What! I thought it was on sale for seventy."

I glare at her. "Plus tax."

She frowns at me. "That's absurd!"

Clankity-clankity-clank.

Dad comes back behind the counter. "Okay, Mrs. Frazier, you're all—"

"Mr. Tibbs, your daughter is trying to charge me over six hundred dollars for that kettle."

Dad's eyebrows smush together as he stares at the register. "Hmm. I don't know how that happened. The kettle is seventy dollars, Mrs. Frazier. Will that be cash or credit?"

"Credit."

Dad clears the cash register, taps in seventy dollars, and then swipes her credit card. The receipt prints, and he gives it to her. "See you in church tomorrow."

My boots can't get me to the back of the store

fast enough. I'm ready to rip open boxes just like Nugget did. My friends are waiting on me when I get there.

"I never knew this store had so much drama," says Starr.

"Total reality show," says Skye.

Nugget interrupts. "Mom would be infuriated with Mrs. Frazier."

Skye shakes her head. "I have no idea what he just said."

"No idea," says Starr.

I walk up to Nugget and frown at him. "I guess kids aren't the only ones who get treated like they don't exist. Did you see how happy Mrs. Frazier was about Mom being out of the cook-off?"

"She totally hated on your mom," says Skye.

"I bet Mrs. Frazier drinks Hater-Ade," says Starr.

"Mya, you've got to do something," says Skye.

"You definitely have to," says Starr.

They're right. The way I see it, Mrs. Frazier is just like Naomi Jackson, except she's a grown-up, and Naomi said things about cowgirls to my face. Mrs. Frazier is talking behind Mom's back. That's total disrespect. There's no way I can let Mrs. Frazier get away with this. Mom is the reigning champ, and I'm her assistant. We deserve a shot at defending our title. And we're going to do it. I'm sure Mom will thank me later.

I drop the supplies back into the box. "I'm entering that chili cook-off."

"What? News flash. You don't know anything about cooking," says Nugget.

"Bad chili can cause red chili bumps, or green chili-itis," says Starr.

"You could die from red chili bumps or green chili-itis," says Skye.

I've never heard of either, but the twins look serious.

"You don't know anything about cooking, and you definitely don't know anything about making chili, except for helping Mom," says Nugget.

"You don't know anything about trying out for baseball, either," I say.

"She's got you there, Nugget," says Skye.

"She's definitely got you," says Starr.

Connie grabs my arm. "What about the Wall of Fame Game? We have to study."

"I know, but I can't just stand here and do nothing. I've got to sign up for that cook-off. Mom's title is at stake. I've got to defend it! Connie, will you go with me? If Mrs. Frazier is there, I might need some help."

"I'm your best friend, and you know I won't leave you hanging," she says.

I hug her. "Okay, let's get these boxes emptied so we can get out of here."

It's boo-yang cool having friends like Connie and the twins. We're working together and getting everything done way faster than if it had been just Nugget and me.

When we finish, we all head for the door. Dad stops me. "Where are you going?"

"To the . . . park," I say.

"What about those Wall of Fame Game questions? Did you bring them like I asked you?"

I reach inside my blue jeans pocket, pull out my questions, and then hand them to Dad. He doesn't waste any time. "Name a famous scientist."

"Albert Einstein."

Dad grins. "Good. Name a Native American tribe."

"Caddo. You should check them out on the internet," I say.

"Awesome, Mya. Last question. How many members are there in the House of Representatives and Senate combined?"

"This one's going to get her," says Starr.

"Got her yesterday," says Skye.

I surprise them both. "There are four hundred and thirty-five members in the House and one hundred in the Senate, so that makes a total of five hundred and thirty-five."

Dad gives me a hug. "Good job! You've got a great jump on the Wall of Fame Game."

I've got a great jump on beating Naomi, but I can't tell Dad that. Right now, I need to kick her and that lame T-shirt out of my mind so I can focus on the cook-off.

"Be back home by two o'clock in case your mother needs you. And thanks for your help today, all of you," says Dad.

Once we're outside, I hug the twins. "You rock. I'll see you at school tomorrow."

Skye takes her sister's hand. Connie and Nugget stand beside me. I feel like an army sergeant. "Nugget, go change into your tryout clothes. Connie and I will be at the park as soon as we can. But right now, I've got to sign up for the chili cook-off before it's too late."

Chapter Eleven

As Connie and I run to Bluebonnet Baptist Church to sign up, I hope I'm not too late. When I open the door, the sound of the choir practicing for tomorrow's service fills my ears with awesome music. They're rocking, clapping, and singing.

"We have to go back there," I say, pointing to a door with *Offices* written on it.

We walk slowly to the door and turn the knob. Inside, a lady sits at a desk with a sign that reads *Last Day to Sign Up for the Chili Cook-Off.* She's very pretty, and I like her red jewelry.

"Can I help you? Your name is Mya, right?"

I look around the office for Mrs. Frazier, hoping she's not hiding behind a trash can or one of those fake plants by the water cooler. When I don't see her, I nod. "Yes, I'm Mya."

"I'm Paula. Do you need some help?"

I take another glance around the place, just to be sure Mrs. Frazier isn't going to jump out from behind a desk or something. "The chili cook-off. I'm here to sign up for—"

Paula smiles. "Of course! Your mom is Monica Tibbs, the reigning champion. Mrs. Frazier will be right back. She's in charge of the cook-off."

My heart pumps double beats. "Wait! Well, couldn't you sign us up this one time? We're kind of in a hurry," I say.

Connie looks at her watch, and then at the door. I don't know if she's worried about Mrs. Frazier, or if she's trying to help me look like I'm short on time.

Paula smiles. "Okay, I can sign you up, no problem."

Connie and I exchange a grin. This could be the best luck I've had all day. Paula keeps talking as she taps on the keyboard.

"And because your mom is the reigning champ,

your entry fee gets waived. Here, fill out this form, and you're all set."

Connie looks at the door again. "When did you say Mrs. Frazier will be back?"

"Any minute now," says Paula.

I write as fast as I can, hoping Mrs. Frazier doesn't show up and bust me.

"Monica Tibbs . . . found her. Oh, and you're listed as her helper! Nice. All right, as soon as you're finished with that form, you can leave," says Paula.

I'm almost at the bottom of the form. My fingers can't write any faster.

And then . . . the door opens.

Connie pulls on my arm. "Oh, no! Hurry up, she's back!"

I sign my name and give the form to Paula. "Thanks so much. The only person who could cancel this would be me or my mom, right?"

"That's right," says the young lady. "And here's your entry receipt. Good luck!"

Mrs. Frazier's eyes are as big as Mom's stomach. She blocks the door. "What's going on here?"

"We're just looking for the restroom and made a wrong turn," says Connie.

We zip around her, open the door, and sprint to

the back of the church. I've been told never to run in church, but I'm hoping that rule is only good on Sundays. Just before we leave, Connie stands in front of a picture of Jesus and folds her hands as if she's praying.

"Sorry about that lie I just told back there in your office. I'll talk to you more about it tonight at bedtime prayers . . . after my parents leave my room. But right now, I've gotta go."

We run down the street without looking back, but deep in my gut, I know what Mrs. Frazier is going to do. Hopefully Mom will listen to me when I get home. Right now, I need to get to the ballpark and root for my brother.

When Connie and I reach the ballpark, we bend over with our hands on our knees as we catch our breath. I stare at the ground and wonder if I just made the biggest mistake on the planet. I've signed up for two huge things in the last three days, and I'm not ready for either one of them. But I do know that Naomi Jackson isn't going to beat me without a good fight, and I won't let Mrs. Frazier beat Mom without one either.

"Micah Tibbs, you're up."

The sound of my brother's name makes me snap

out of my thoughts and remember where I am. "Connie, let's go! We can't miss Nugget's tryout."

We sit on the first bench of the bleachers. Even though I want to root for my brother, the faces of Naomi and Mrs. Frazier circle my brain like sharks. I have to get rid of them. So I stand and shout good things to my brother. But it comes out all wrong.

"Crush that ball, Naomi!"

Good gravy.

Connie stares at me as I slowly take a seat.

"She's not here."

I frown. "Yes, she is, and I can't get her out of my head."

Connie unzips her backpack. "I know Nugget was in a bad mood at the store. Maybe if I draw a picture of him whacking a home run, he'll feel better."

My brother rushes out of the dugout. Coach frowns at him. "Where's your gear, Tibbs?"

Nugget touches his hair. "Oh, right, I need a helmet! Sorry, Coach."

Nugget's dressed in blue shorts and a T-shirt Dad bought him at the Children's Science Store that reads *Never Trust an Atom. They Make Up Everything.* Must've been on sale because they misspelled Adam. Why is Nugget wearing his sandals?

I stand and clap before he bats. "Hit the ball, Nugget!"

"Come on, Nugget! I'm going to draw a picture of you hitting the ball!" yells Connie.

He holds the bat high. The pitch comes in fast. Nugget swings and misses. The second pitch comes in. He misses again. When Coach throws the third pitch, Nugget hits the ball, but it's more of a baby tap, since it barely rolls back to the pitcher. When Coach Booker throws the next ball, Nugget swings so hard that the bat hits him in the back of the head.

Clunk.

"Ouch!"

I knew it.

Connie lets out a big sigh. "He didn't really give me anything to draw."

"Tibbs, go to left field!" yells Coach. "Here comes a fly ball."

Nugget holds his glove up, moves to the left, to the right, and then . . .

Plop.

He picks up the ball and throws it back toward the infield.

Running drills are a little better. He doesn't finish first, but he isn't last, either.

Soon tryouts are over. Connie and I stay quiet as Nugget unlocks his bike from the rack. I can't take the silence anymore.

"So, what did the coach say?"

"Tomorrow he's going to post the roster on the bulletin board near the concession stand over there. Everybody who tried out made the team," says Nugget.

"Yay! Wait . . . so if everybody made the team, why have a tryout?" I ask.

"So Coach can see who's good at catching, batting, throwing, running—you know, things like that. It will help him figure out our positions on the field." He swallows hard. "Tryouts were a lot harder than I thought they would be." He stares at his sandals. "I don't know why I wore these. Let's go home."

"Those are nice sandals. I'm going to go home and study," says Connie.

I hug my friend. "I'll call you later. Thanks for going with me to sign up for the cook-off."

I'm almost jogging trying to keep up with my brother as he walks his bike home.

"Why aren't you happy? You made the team. That's all that matters, right?"

He shakes his head. "What if I don't get any

better, Mya? Instead of proving Dad wrong, I proved him right. I stink at baseball! Did you see how badly I missed that easy pop-up in the outfield? It landed right next to my feet. Dad and I are never going to do things like Fish and his dad. That's because I'm a loser."

Chapter Twelve

I wish I knew what to say to make Nugget feel better about his tryout, but I can tell he's not in a talking mood. I'm glad because I need to get upstairs and look over my questions again. Naomi's probably got the whole study sheet memorized by now.

Nugget lets his bike fall in the front yard. He never does that. I pick it up and push the kickstand down. He can thank me later.

I know we're in trouble as soon as we walk in the door. With his arms folded across his chest, Dad gives us a firm look. "Where have you two been? It's two forty-five!"

I point, like that's going to help. "We were over . . . wait. See, we went . . . and then we . . . remember, I told you we were going . . . okay, let me tell you what happened."

Dad's got all kinds of mad in his face. "The last thing your mother needs right now is to be worried about where her children are!"

Mom's feet rest on a fluffy pillow on the otto-man. She looks down and rubs her belly.

My brother yells, "I went to try out for baseball!"

His words echo off the walls in the living room.

Dad's head tilts to one side. "Why didn't you tell me?"

Nugget doesn't wait for Dad to finish. He rushes up the stairs. "I just wanted to prove to you that I could make the team! Fish's dad takes him to Burger Bar for breakfast! You've never taken me to the Burger Bar for breakfast. I bet Solo's dad takes him, too!"

"So this is about breakfast?" asks Dad.

Nugget runs to his room and closes the door.

Dad turns to Mom and me. One part of his face looks surprised, while another part is still frown-ing from when we walked in. "How did this end up being about me? Did I miss something?" he asks.

"Just let him cool down," says Mom. "I'm sure

you remember what tryouts were like."

Dad sighs. "Yes, I do. That's why I don't understand why he didn't talk to me first. Anyway, I'm going to Macey's room to put her crib together. Yell if you need me."

I ease over to the sofa, take a seat, and keep my mouth shut. Neither Mom nor Dad has said my name since Dad asked, "Where have you two been?" So I'm feeling pretty good. I even slap a grin on my face and look Mom's way.

"Mya, I just got off the phone with Mrs. Frazier."

That has to have been the shortest grin in the history of grins.

Good gravy.

Mom's got that same tilt to her head that Dad had when he was talking to Nugget. I grip the sofa cushions and hold on. I don't know if she's going to punish me or make me go back to the church and apologize to Mrs. Frazier. But first she needs to hear my side.

"Did Mrs. Frazier tell you about what she said at our store, on our store property, around our store stuff?"

"No she didn't," says Mom. "She just wanted to make sure I knew you had signed us up for the cookoff. What's going on?"

I cross my arms over my chest. "Did she ask how you were feeling? Did she ask about Macey? Did she even give you any advice for swollen ankles?"

Mom shakes her head. "No. We weren't on the phone very long."

I put my hands on my hips and stand. "Mrs. Frazier is not your friend, Mom! I'm an expert in having friends that aren't really your friends. When Dad told Mrs. Frazier that you weren't going to be in the chili cook-off, she smiled, and then she got on her cell and blasted the news all over Bluebonnet like she was happy! Is that what a real friend would do? I don't think so. Even with swollen ankles, I bet your chili would beat hers."

Mom's still frowning. "But I told you I wasn't going to compete this year, Mya. Then you deliberately went behind my back and signed us up anyway."

Without thinking, I blurt out, "What else was I supposed to do?"

Mom sits up. "What?"

My bottom lip trembles. I blink hard, hoping the tears stay away, but they don't listen to me. I try to explain the best I can.

"We're in the chili cook-off every year. Now all of sudden we're not. Then Mrs. Frazier started talking about how happy she was that you weren't going to be in the contest, right there in our store as if . . . as if I was invisible! Like it didn't matter that I was standing there! It just seems like . . . I got so mad because . . . everything is getting canceled, and it's not fair."

I want to tell Mom that I'm scared that I'm going to be invisible to her, too, but my words won't come out. So I just stop talking. Mom nods and stretches out an arm for me to come to her. I put my head on her shoulder, and she leans hers against mine as she wipes the tears from my face. We sit in silence for a long time.

"Tomorrow, after church, I want you to go straight upstairs and study your Wall of Fame Game questions, and then bring them to me so I can quiz you."

I let out a big mouthful of air. "But Dad already quizzed me on them."

Mom smiles. "Good! Then you shouldn't have any trouble when I quiz you! After that, we'll switch over to the kitchen for one hour. When it comes to cooking, you've got lots of things to learn, like measurements and temperature, and how long something should cook. You have to take your time and be patient. Making a mistake with any of those things could completely ruin your meal. And Mya . . . making prize-winning chili has nothing to do with winning a prize."

"Huh? Then why would you even bother?" I ask.

Mom sits up. "I'll let you tell me that at the end of the week. Because this year, I'm not making the chili. You are."

I think about what Mom said all day Saturday. I even think about it in church on Sunday morning. I ask God to forgive Connie for lying yesterday, and to forgive me if I make bad chili and someone gets red chili bumps or green chili-itis. What if people end up barfing in the grass near the Little League fields because they ate my chili?

Maybe I'm thinking too much. Or maybe it's this itchy church dress that's got me all uncomfortable. And these white tights made me scratch a rip so big that my knee sticks out like the top of Mount Everest. I'm sure both this dress and these tights are made out of mosquito bites.

After church, I change clothes and study some of the Wall of Fame Game questions that I haven't studied before. I know the answers for tomorrow already, so I might as well try to memorize some of the other ones. I go to the nightstand next to my bed, grab my clock, and place it next to my computer. Then I close my eyes and point to a question on the study sheet. When I open my eyes, I know I'm in trouble.

Name five countries in Europe. Good gravy. I know France is over there, and Hungary, and Russia. How many is that? Firecrackers! I'm never going to get these answers right. Naomi's going to crush me.

I march to my mirror, put my hands on my hips, frown at my reflection in the mirror, and go off on myself. "She challenged you! Naomi called Annie Oakley a baby show! And she said beauty pageant winners are smarter than cowgirls. Well then—bring it, missy!"

Mom calls to me. "Are you ready for me to quiz you?"

I grab my sheet. "I sure am! Here I come."

I stand in front of her as she asks me the questions. I go three for three and get a super-duper hug. I close my eyes as Mom holds me. It feels wonderful.

"Keep studying, and do the best you can. Your dad and I are so proud of you and Nugget. With your brother trying out for baseball, and you signing up for the Wall of Fame Game, and the chili cook-off, both of you are going to be stronger and more dedicated young people."

I smile, because now I know Nugget and I did the right things. Signing up for baseball and the chili cook-off means Mom and Dad will not forget about us. My reasons for taking on the Wall of Fame Game have nothing to do with my family. They don't need to know that.

Knock, knock.

The front door opens. "It's me . . . Connie. Can I come in?"

"Sure!"

"Hi, Mrs. Tibbs." Connie takes her backpack off her shoulders. "Mya and I are going to study. We're ready for tomorrow, but we're going to try and memorize the harder questions that will come later in the week. We need to figure out how we're going to do that."

Mom gives a thumbs-up. "Good plan!"

I lead the way to the stairs and into my room. Connie's already talking about study plans.

"You don't need a study buddy for Monday's Wall of Fame Game answers, but Tuesday, each question will have two answers. Three questions means six answers."

"I need a study buddy every day if I'm going to beat the ba-jeebies out of Naomi Jackson. I've got to know the answers like I know my own name. I'm sure Naomi has someone helping her study like that."

Connie smiles at me. "I need a study buddy too. We're perfect for each other!"

I hug my best friend. "Okay, I don't want to talk about the Wall of Fame Game right now. You're not going to believe what happened yesterday before I got home. Mrs. Frazier called."

Connie puts down her study sheet. "She is so mean."

"Mom wasn't happy, but I told her what Mrs. Frazier did, and you know what? I think she totally understood, because guess what—I'm making the chili this year, all by myself!"

Connie's eyes widen. "No way!"

I nod. "Yes, way! I get my first cooking lesson on kitchen safety in just a few minutes. Wanna come? Mom's going to show me what she knows, and then I'm taking it from there. Is that the coolest thing or what? Mrs. Frazier's chili doesn't stand a chance against chili made by the Magnificent Mya Tibbs!"

Chapter Thirteen

When Connie and I rush downstairs for our first cooking lesson, it's very quiet. I check Mom's room. She's asleep. That's okay, because by making this chili, I'm going to remind her how much fun we have together. I close her door and head to the kitchen.

There're several bowls on the counter, and each bowl is covered with a napkin. I know what that is, and it makes me smile.

"Mom chopped up my ingredients for me! Boo-yang!"

Connie peeks underneath each napkin. "You put

all this stuff in your chili? Our chili just needs a can opener. No wonder you win."

Connie and I wash our hands, and I set the recipe on the counter. I figure if I throw some of each ingredient in a microwaveable bowl, that will do it, since this is just a test.

I read the recipe. "Hey, Connie, do you know what T-S-P or T-B-S-P stands for? It's everywhere on this paper. And have you ever heard of a dollop? I know what a wallop is, but not a dollop."

Connie puts her finger over her lips. "Let's see, you beat eggs, and mash potatoes, but I can't think of a food you're supposed to wallop. That's why I only make ham-and-cheese sandwiches for me and Clayton. No violence."

I shrug. "When Mom and I make chili, my job is to put all the spices on the counter in alphabetical order. She asks for one, I hand it to her, and just for fun, I play the name game. Here's how you play. For example, if Mom asked me for parsley, I'd have to use the letter P for a first name, a place where I live, and the kind of job I have. So maybe I'd say, 'My name is Paul, I live in Pittsburgh, and I sell parsley."

Connie straightens out the spices. "That sounds like fun!"

"It is, but I never did any measuring. It can't be that hard."

I'm still scratching my head about these initials. "Maybe T-S-P stands for 'the salt and pepper' and T-B-S-P stands for 'tiny bit of salt and pepper.' Makes sense to me."

Connie shrugs. "Me, too. Okay, here's the salt, and I want to play the game. My name is Sophie, I live in Switzerland, and I sell salt for a living!"

She giggles, and so do I. This is going to be fun. I'm adding salt, pepper, chili powder, and other ingredients as if I were Mom. And then, the absolute weirdest ingredient pops up.

"What does one clove from a knob of garlic mean?"

Connie checks the recipe. "You mean, like a doorknob knob, or a kitchen cabinet knob? Geez, Mya. Dollops and knobs? Seems like you'd find those in a hardware store. At my house, our garlic is in a jar, and it's called minced garlic, not knob garlic. I've heard of cloves. It's totally different than garlic. They don't even smell the same. That's got to be a mistake."

I check the refrigerator and spot a jar of minced garlic. "Okay, I think I'm on to something." Connie and I stare at the jar and then at the recipe before

I shake my head. "How am I supposed to make a doorknob out of this?"

And then my best friend comes up with the best idea ever. "Let's just forget about the clove part, because I think it may be a typo on the recipe. Maybe if I can get a big handful of that minced garlic, and squeeze the juice off, I can shape it into a knob. That would make sense."

Connie makes a bowl with her left hand, pours the whole jar of garlic into it, and then squeezes her hand into a tight fist. Garlic juice seeps and drips between her fingers and into the sink.

"Hurry up, Connie. That's going to make me barf," I say.

She's pushing and pinching the garlic in her hand. "I'm trying really hard, but it won't hold together," says Connie.

I shrug. "But I think you've got a knob of it, don't you?"

She nods. "Oh, yeah, this is definitely enough garlic to make a knob."

"Then let's just dump it in the bowl and turn the microwave on. We've got to get back to studying."

Seeing all the onions, garlic, bell peppers, chili meat, diced tomatoes, and tomato sauce in the bowl brings back more memories of Mom and me during the chili cook-off. We'd get to the booth early on Saturday morning, before the cook-off started. I'd hand her vegetables, and she'd chop them up as we'd talk about everything. She'd have a thermos of hot coffee, and she'd make me one full of hot chocolate.

My memory ends, and I stare at the microwave. Mom usually cooks this on the stove for four hours, but I'm not allowed to turn on the burners. So, to make up the difference in time, I set the microwave for two hours, since it cooks stuff faster than a stove.

When Connie and I get back to my room, I leave the door open so I can hear the ding of the microwave. I've got everything going that I need to beat Naomi and Mrs. Frazier! Soon Connie and I are quizzing each other on more Wall of Fame Game questions, and getting surprised when we give the right answers. To celebrate, I turn on the radio and teach her how to do the Mya Shuffle, a new two-step I made up.

"Take two steps to the right, lift your left leg, and tap your left heel with your right hand twice. Take two steps to the left, lift your right leg, and tap your right heel with your left hand twice. Good. Now heel, toe, stomp, with your right foot. Heel, toe, stomp with your left foot, and gallop on your horse like Annie Oakley as you turn to the left! Atta girl! You did it!"

Connie keeps going. "That's fun! Come on, Mya, I want to do it again."

I stop dancing. "Do you smell something burning?"

BEEEEEEP!!! BEEEEEEP!!! BEEEEEEP!!!

"What's going on? That's the smoke alarm!" I say.

Our eyes open wider than the top on a can of beans as we say together, "THE CHILI!"

Connie and I rush downstairs to the kitchen. Mom's running water in a bowl that has lots of smoke coming out of it. There's no happy in Mom's face as thick black goo *gluck-gluck-gluck*s out of the bowl and then down the sink.

Mom points to the window. "Mya, open that all the way to help get rid of this smoke. Connie, take this dish towel and fan the alarm to push the smoke away," she says.

I rush to the window and open it. Connie grabs a dish towel and waves it to clear the smoke. Mom taps the reset button, and the alarm goes quiet.

Mom points to the dining room. "Go sit at the table and wait for me. You could have burned the house down."

"Mom, I'm so sorry," I say.

Connie looks like she's going to cry. "Sorry, Mrs. Tibbs."

As we sit and listen to Mom scrub that bowl both of my knees bounce, and I can't stop them. Maybe that's my body trying to show me how fast a fire would have moved through our house! I could have cooked my whole family.

The house smells worse than burned popcorn, and it's all my fault. For the first time in my life, I realize the kitchen is a dangerous place. I thought I had everything under control. I thought I could cook and study at the same time. I thought making chili was going to be easy.

Mom grimaces as she slowly waddles to the table. Some of that frown may be from her swollen ankles hurting, but I'm sure most of it is from what I just did. She holds her stomach as if she's already holding Macey in her arms. My eyes lower toward her ankles. It makes me hurt to look at them. As soon as she sits, I help her prop her legs up on a chair.

"Mya, you've got lots of things to learn about cooking in the kitchen. We are all very lucky. That could have been a deadly mistake."

"I'm really sorry, Mom."

"I'll never help do that again without your permission, Mrs. Tibbs," says Connie.

Mom looks at my best friend. "Connie, are you Mya's assistant this year?"

Connie shrugs. "Since I assisted in almost burning your house down, I guess so."

I've got the best friend in the world. She doesn't back away from trouble. She doesn't mind standing with me, even when things don't turn out the right way.

"You're an awesome assistant," I tell her, and then turn to Mom. "Okay. I want to know everything, because we're going to beat Mrs. Frazier, right?"

I glance at the clock on the dining-room wall. I hope Mom doesn't talk a long time, because Mrs. Frazier isn't the only person I plan to beat this week. "Is this going to take long? Connie and I need to study our Wall of Fame Game questions."

"You can't rush cooking, Mya. It's about patience, and taking your time. Those things can't change. And you have to learn your way around the kitchen."

"But if you help me like you did today, by cutting up all the veggies, and cooking the chili meat for me, than that will make it so much easier. Thanks, Mom."

"I can't help you on Saturday, Mya," says Mom. "You'll have to do everything yourself. First, let's learn how to use measuring tools in the kitchen."

I feel like my plan to do something with Mom just burned up with the chili. She loves to cook, and I was sure once she smelled my spices and vegetables cooking together, it would make her want to join me. And my plan would have worked, too, because we'd be doing something together. When she told me I'd be making the chili by myself, I didn't think she was serious.

I was wrong.

For a whole hour, Mom goes over and over how tsp, or just the lowercase "t," means teaspoon, and tbsp, or the capital letter "T," means tablespoon. She teaches us about quarts and pints, a third of this and three-fourths of that. We know a clove of garlic is just a piece of a whole one, which is also called a knob. Then she makes me repeat it back. This isn't fun. This isn't even close to what I wanted. Mom's teaching me her job. I want *her* to do it. I want *us* to make the chili together.

It's just like watching westerns and going to Open House by myself. I'm still going to be invisible to Mom, and now I'm stuck making chili without her, too.

Chapter Fourteen

On Monday, I can still smell burned chili downstairs from the microwave mess I made yesterday. I smelled it while I was dreaming last night, too. I thought all night about whether or not I should just drop out of the chili cook-off since Mom's not going to help me.

But I'm no quitter. I argued hard with her just to stay in the cook-off. And even though she won't be helping me make chili, I don't ever want to hurt her feelings, especially over something she loves to do.

I sit on the edge of my bed this morning, figuring things out and getting myself pumped up for the

day. I'm feeling pretty good about everything . . .
until that tiara-wearing turkey's face pops up in my
brain. My fists ball, and my toes curl just thinking about her. Naomi Jackson insulted the entire
cowgirl nation, and I'm going to make her eat those
words. I get dressed faster than I ever have before.
I'm on a mission, and it starts today.

I ask Mom to make me one thick ponytail,
because even though I have three questions for the
Wall of Fame Game, each question only gets one
answer. I go over them in my head while she makes
my braid. The ruffle of newspapers breaks my concentration. When I see where it's coming from, I
shake my head.

Nugget and Dad sit at opposite ends of the table,
eating breakfast and reading parts of the paper.
They're not talking, just reading. They didn't wrestle for the newspaper this morning like they usually
do. Ever since Nugget announced he tried out for
the baseball team, they haven't said much of anything to each other.

After I eat, Nugget's ready to go, so I get my
backpack and follow him outside. As we walk to
school, he kicks a rock and talks to me.

"Dad showed up at my practice yesterday. He sat
in the stands with Mr. Leatherwood and watched us

for about ten minutes and then left. Ten minutes! I figured if I made the team, we'd do stuff like Fish does with his dad. I thought he'd at least come watch me practice. But he only stayed ten minutes. I don't even know why he bothered to come. He didn't talk to me. I just happened to see him standing next to Mr. Leatherwood."

"At least he came for a little while. Maybe that's all the time he had. Did he see you bat?"

"I struck out. That's what he saw. And then he left. I'm not the only player who strikes out a lot. My team stinks like our house." Nugget's face wrinkles like he's got a mouthful of Lemonheads. "Speaking of stink, do you know what that smell is that's coming from the kitchen?"

Instead of answering, I change the subject. "Why does your team stink?"

"Everybody stinks except Fish and Solo. They're really good. But the rest of us, if Coach threw a curveball or anything other than a fastball, we couldn't hit it. I can tell what the pitcher's going to throw, but I just can't seem to hit that ball!"

"You just need more practice, that's all," I say, hoping I said the right thing.

We spot Fish ahead of us. He waits with a big grin. "Happy Dictionary Day, Mya Papaya!"

"Dictionary Day. That's a good one, Fish," I say.

Nugget nods. "Good ol' Noah Webster. He's the guy who came up with the dictionary back in the 1700s."

I'm glad Fish is here because Nugget was getting sadder, and it was making me feel sad, too. I need to be pumped up and excited about today. Being sad could mess me up.

As soon as I open the school door, music blares from the intercom and flips my mood from excited to nervous. This is it. The road to beating Naomi starts right here.

The hall sounds like a stampede is coming, but it's just a herd of boys nearby. Nugget and Fish nod at me and then head to their classroom. I shuffle toward mine. Mrs. Davis smiles as I pass her desk.

"Good morning, Mya! Are you ready for the Wall of Fame Game?"

I give her a thumbs-up on my way to my cabinet. "Yes, ma'am, I am!"

It's hot in the cave. Maybe because it's so crowded. Students sit on the floor, stand by their cabinets, face the wall, or pair up with someone as they go over their Wall of Fame Game questions. Some bang a cabinet when they answer wrong, or give high fives and fist bumps for encouragement. Some wipe their foreheads, while others take swigs of water from plastic bottles. Geez. It's just three questions and three answers today. I guess they didn't study.

The air's definitely different in here. It feels thick, like it's filled with fear. I go over the answers in my head.

"Are you ready?"

I glance over my shoulder. Naomi's behind me, dressed in a pretty red top with blue-and-red shorts. Even her shoes are red. Since she didn't ask me in a mean way, I answer her in my regular voice.

"Yes, I'm ready. Are you?"

She rolls her eyes. "Of course. I have a lot at stake, and I'm not even talking about the bet you're going to lose. I need to make the wall for my career, so judges and maybe movie directors will know that I'm also very smart, which is so much more important than whatever your reason might be."

I won't let her make me nervous, since *she's* the reason I'm going to make the wall. So I get up and *ka-clunk* to my desk without saying another word.

After the Pledge of Allegiance, Mr. Winky wishes all the fourth graders good luck as he finishes the announcements.

The door opens, and Mrs. Hansen, our librarian, walks in. "Good morning, class."

"Good morning, Mrs. Hansen," we all say together.

Mrs. Davis opens her desk drawer and pulls out a clipboard, an egg timer, and a pen. She stands and walks to the cave as Mrs. Hansen takes a seat at her desk.

"When I call your name, please follow me into the cave. David?"

He rises from his seat and walks behind Mrs. Davis. We all watch him as if we'll never see him again. I've got a clear view of the cave. There's a curtain in the very back that pulls from the right to the left. They go behind it.

Mrs. Hansen clears her throat. "Okay, class, let's talk about writing a mystery. What kinds of things go in a mystery story?"

Michael raises his hand. "A crime."

Mrs. Hansen writes that on the board. "Very good. What else?"

There's no movement behind the curtain. I wonder if David fainted. I'm exactly twelve students away from passing out just like him.

Ding!

I think I heard the egg timer go off in the cave. When I look around, others are staring at the cave, too. The room is silent again. David appears from behind the curtain, walking faster than he did going in. Everyone's looking at him, hoping to catch a clue from his expression or a thumbs-up or something. He sits down and looks straight ahead. I know that look.

He missed one. Now he's got to be perfect for the rest of the week, or he's done.

Mrs. Davis calls the next student to her doom. "Susan?"

Susan Acorn pushes back in her chair and heads to the front of the class. We all watch her the same way we watched David. Even Mrs. Hansen is watching. Once I hear the *zip* of the curtain closing, I can't help but worry about my brain staying ready until it's my turn.

I glance over at Naomi. There are five kids before her. I hope when it's her turn to go into the cave, she misses all three questions and ends this bet today.

"What else do you need in a mystery?" asks Mrs. Hansen.

I can't think about mysteries right now. My eyes ping-pong from Naomi to the cave. One by one, my classmates go in looking scared. But when they come out, it's as if they're under a spell, stuck in stupid, like all of the smart got sucked out of their brain.

"Naomi?"

She walks down the aisle like it's a runway and she's in a beauty pageant. I think about sticking out my boot to trip her, but I don't want to get scuff marks on my pretty pink kickers. Soon she strolls out the same way she went in, with a three-out-of-three look on her face.

Just wait until it's my turn. Naomi wants to stroll into the cave like a beauty queen? Then I'm going to *ka-clunk* in like Annie Oakley. And when it's over, I hope I can flash a three-out-of-three smile just like she did.

Chapter Fifteen

The Wall of Fame Game has been going on for an hour. Mrs. Davis gives us a restroom break, and I can't wait to talk to some of my classmates who have already been asked their Wall of Fame Game questions. I catch David before he goes in the boys' restroom.

"You didn't look so good when you came out of the cave," I say.

"It's over. I totally froze in there. Missed all three questions. My heart was pounding and I couldn't breathe. It was a nightmare. Good luck, Mya."

"Sorry, David," I say.

I find the twins standing by a sink in the rest-room. Starr's brushing Skye's hair. I try to keep my voice down. "So, how'd you do?"

Skye nods. "I started crying, and then I started laughing, and told Mrs. Davis that the only reason I signed up was because my sister signed up. She put down her clipboard, and I told her about all the false alien spaceship sightings this year, and why our parents created the extended-lens telescope. I had a very nice visit with her in the cave."

Skye and Starr's parents own Bluebonnet Hunting Gear and Observatory next door to Tibbs's Farm and Ranch Store. I think they know more about aliens than the FBI.

"I studied Skye's questions by accident, so I got disqualified," says Starr with a shrug.

Skye nods. "But you don't have anything to worry about, Mya. You're one of the smartest girls in our class. Starr and I think you're going to get a perfect score."

I open the door. "I have to. I think Naomi went three for three. Thanks."

Inside the classroom, I walk straight to my desk and throw my leg over my chair like it's the saddle for a Clydesdale. Michael sits in front of me, with his head down on his desk.

"You're not sick, are you?" I ask.

He turns around and smiles. "Who, me? I'm cool as a cucumber."

I don't think cucumbers are cool. They're a vegetable, and that's it.

As soon as everyone's back from the restroom, Mrs. Davis calls the next name.

"Michael?"

He tucks his shirt into his pants and runs his hand over his hair, as if how he looks will make a difference in his score. It feels like he's only gone for a few seconds when . . .

Ding!

Michael's face is hot-sauce red when he comes out of the cave. Something bad is happening back there. First David, then the twins, now Michael. My heart thumps so hard that it's shaking my whole body.

"Mya?"

I try to walk like I normally do, but my steps are all messed up. It's as if my boots lost their *ka-clunk*. I feel like I'm going to fall on my face at any moment.

Mrs. Davis smiles when I reach her. "Ready?"

My tongue is stuck to the roof of my mouth. All I can do is nod. As we walk to the back of the cave, my stomach's turning flips and my brain is already searching for answers that haven't been asked yet. I try to take a big breath and let it out slowly, but that's not working.

When Mrs. Davis slides the curtain closed, the space is so small that I can barely breathe. She pulls out a paper that has my name on the top. "Here we go."

She taps the egg timer. "Name a famous scientist."

I close my eyes and focus. "Albert Einstein."

"Correct. How many members in the Senate and House of Representatives combined?"

"There are one hundred members in the Senate, and four hundred and thirty-five in the House of Representatives. So that equals five hundred and thirty-five all together."

Mrs. Davis winks at me. "Atta girl! Last question. Name a Native American tribe."

"Caddo. Hey, Mrs. Davis, did you know the Caddo tribe has been in Texas for over a thousand years? I read online they actually came up with our state's name! It was Taysha, and that means friend. I like that, don't you? Texas people are friendly."

Ding.

"And one more thing, Mrs. Davis, I was reading

about Albert Einstein since I chose him as my scientist, and listen to what he once said." I take my right boot off and turn it upside down. A piece of paper falls out, and I grab it from the floor. "I wrote it down so I wouldn't mess it up when I told you. He said, 'Look deep into nature, and then you will understand everything better.' I think Mr. Einstein was a cowboy, because cowboys love being on nature trails."

Mrs. Davis smiles. "Where did you read that quote from Albert Einstein?"

"He's got a Twitter page."

Mrs. Davis giggles. "Well, I'm happy to hear that you're enjoying the Wall of Fame Game."

I shrug. "I wouldn't say I'm enjoying it, but I am learning about a lot of things that I can add to my taradiddles."

Mrs. Davis shrugs, but then smiles. "Mya Tibbs, you answered all three questions correctly. That means you are eligible to continue the Wall of Fame Game tomorrow."

"Oh, yeah, that's right!" I feel like there are rockets on the heels of my boots! I didn't cry. I didn't freeze! I got them right, and I'm moving on to Tuesday. Yee-haw!

Ka-clunk, ka-clunk, ka-clunk.

All eyes are on me when I step back into the classroom. I refuse to look at Naomi. But I glance at Connie and whisper, "Yippee-ki-yay!"

When it's Connie's turn, my knee gets nervous and jumpy from the moment she follows Mrs. Davis until they both come out of the cave. Connie whispers as she goes by, "Three out of three!" My knee stops jumping, and I whisper, "Boo-yang!"

For the rest of the day, I wonder what tomorrow's questions are going to be. I'm hoping they'll be as easy as the ones I had today. But right before the after-school bell rings, Mrs. Davis hands out our Tuesday Wall of Fame Game questions. Holy ravioli.

WALL OF FAME GAME QUESTIONS FOR MYA TIBBS:

TUESDAY

1. Name two fruits that do not grow on trees.
2. Name two inventors and their inventions.
3. Name two birds that can't fly.

I hope Connie can come over right after school. I need to get studying as soon as possible. And I can't forget the chili. No more burning the house down. In five days, the cook-off is going to happen with or without me, and Mom's title is on the line. I've got to get that recipe right.

Chapter Sixteen

After school, Connie and I walk, talk, and re-live every moment of our our time in the cave with Mrs. Davis. We talk about the ticking of the egg timer, the questions, and how nervous we were. Fish and Nugget are up ahead, but we want to be by ourselves, so we walk slower.

We're fist-bumping, and giggling, and making plans for our study time this afternoon. I figure this is the perfect time for a taradiddle.

"My boots had a sparkle on the tip, right before I went back in the cave for my Wall of Fame Game questions. The sparkle rushed up my legs, my arms, my neck, and all the way to my head. I knew it was Annie Oakley, coming all the way to Bluebonnet to help me. I'm sure that's why I went three for three."

Connie rolls her eyes. "Annie Oakley in Bluebonnet? I don't think so. You and your taradiddles, Mya."

"I wonder how Naomi did. She acted like she got everything right, but I don't know for sure. I'll keep the pressure on her. I'm going to get another perfect score tomorrow. And today we have to do a better job with the chili," I say.

"Now that we know what a clove from a knob of garlic is, and that T-S-P doesn't have anything to do with salt and pepper unless you measure them, we should do a better job," says Connie.

"Right. As long as we remember there are ten cloves in a knob of garlic, we'll be fine. That's going to make a big difference."

We must be walking faster than Fish and my brother because soon we're right behind them, and I hear Fish going off.

"You're thinking about your dad so much that you can't swing the bat! Just relax. You can do it. I know you can, bro."

Nugget shakes his head. "You don't have the same problem I've got, Fish. You crush the ball every time you come to the plate. My dad can't say a thing about your game."

Fish gets louder. "Look, we should be having fun playing on the same team. You're letting your dad get in your head and ruin everything."

"Yeah, maybe so. But sometimes a guy's got to prove himself. Let's cross the street here," says Nugget. "See you later, Mya. Later, Connie."

Fish nods our way, and then rushes to catch up with my brother.

I wait until I'm sure the boys can't hear me. "Connie, let's go over to the ballpark. I'm getting worried about my brother. We can hide under the bleachers and see what's going on."

She nods. "I think that's a good idea. But we can't stay long."

"I know. I can't study to beat Naomi if I'm sitting at a ballpark. I wonder if she's already studying. She wasn't in the cave very long at all answering her questions. I mean, did you notice what time she left her desk and what time she got back?"

"I didn't notice," says Connie.

"Seemed like less than a minute."

As we get closer to the park, Connie and I hide behind trees, trash cans, anything we can to make sure we don't get busted for spying. Finally we make it to the bleachers, but then I notice Dad is sitting with Mr. Leatherwood. I'm supposed to go straight home after school, so I don't want Dad to see me. Connie and I tiptoe back behind the tree and watch from there.

Coach has the players taking hitting practice. Solo's up first. The coach is pitching, and he whizzes one right past Solo. "Strike one!"

Nugget stands nearby and watches everything Coach does on the mound.

"What's Nugget doing? Why isn't he in the dugout with the other players?" whispers Connie.

"I'm not sure," I whisper back.

Coach throws another heater. Solo swings and misses. "That's two!"

Suddenly Nugget runs toward Solo. "Time out!"

Coach yells, "Tibbs, get back in the dugout!"

Nugget holds up a finger. "I just need to tell Solo something."

"Make it fast!" says Coach.

Nugget whispers something to Solo, who's nodding as they both look back at Coach standing on the mound. Soon Solo gives Nugget a fist bump. Then my brother trots back to the dugout. Coach hollers to Solo.

"Okay, here comes the pitch."

Coach throws. Solo holds his bat high and waits. *Smack!*

Connie jumps like it scared her. "Geez, Mya! That ball's going over the fence!"

Nugget's teammates wait for Solo at home plate. They jump and holler. Solo gives Nugget a high five. Nugget pats him on the helmet before the two of them jog back to the dugout together.

Three batters later, Fish comes to the plate and hits one to the outfield. The batter on second base comes home, and Fish ends up on second base. Mr. Leatherwood whistles and claps. I clap too, until Connie grabs my hands.

"We're not supposed to be here, remember?"

"Oh, right! I forgot. Anyway, it's Nugget's turn." I close my eyes and cross my fingers. *Please, please hit the ball.*

Coach throws three fast pitches. Nugget swings and misses all of them, then throws his bat down and stomps to the dugout. Coach blows his whistle.

"Tibbs! Get back out here and pick up that bat! Then you can run two laps around the field for attitude. Don't let me see you acting like that again!"

Dad steps down the bleachers and walks to his truck. Soon he's heading back to work.

"I think we'd better go," I say.

"Yeah, this is a good time to leave," says Connie.

On the way to my house, I can't help but think out loud. "I'm not sure what Nugget whispered to Solo, but whatever it was helped Solo smack a home run. So why can't Nugget hit a home run? I'd be happy if his bat just accidentally touched the ball."

"I was thinking the same thing, but I don't know enough about baseball to even have a conversation like that with myself."

"Me either. But the way he threw down that bat . . . I'm getting really worried about him."

Chapter Seventeen

I'm not going to mention to Nugget what I saw at the baseball field today. I'm not a low-down dirty rat, and neither is Connie. If Dad wants to talk to Nugget about it, he can mention it, but I won't.

When we get home, Connie and I go straight to Mom's room. She's sitting on her couch reading with her feet up on the ottoman. She pats the cushion for us to take a seat with her. "So, how was the first day of the Wall of Fame Game?" she asks.

Connie and I talk at the same time, and then we tell each other to go ahead and talk, and then we talk at the same time again! I begin to tell Mom something about the Wall of Fame Game, and Connie finishes my sentences! It's funny, but it feels so good that both of us went three for three today.

"Mom, we have to study. Is there anything special you want to tell me about making chili today?"

She nods. "I put all the ingredients out again, but this time you have to chop them up yourself with that Kitchen Kid's safe-blade chopper. Do you remember how to use it?"

"Of course," I say. "It's easy-peasy! I've used it at least ten times since you bought it."

"Good. It will help you chop your veggies into small, perfect pieces. Take your time, and do it right. Your father brought home five individual packs of precooked hamburger crumbles. That is going to be your chili meat to practice with. You can only make one practice bowl in the microwave a day, so make it the best you can."

"I promise we'll watch the bowl this time, Mom."

She nods. "Let me know as soon as you turn the microwave on."

Connie and I unload our backpacks on the dining-room table. I bring my computer downstairs and plug it in. This is where we'll work this week so that we can study and make chili in the same place. I get my questions out.

"I bet Naomi hasn't memorized any of her answers yet. She'll probably miss one tomorrow. You know, Connie, Naomi's really not that smart."

Connie lets out a big sigh. "Will you please stop talking about her? I'm trying to study."

"I can't help it. Beating her is all I can think about."

I plop down at the table and turn on the computer. I already decided on blueberries and watermelons as my fruits that don't grow on trees. That wasn't hard at all. But finding inventors makes me go to the internet.

I definitely want women inventors. Oh, check this out! I'm choosing Mary Anderson because she invented the windshield wiper for cars. I bet a whole lot of people don't know that! And I'll take Marion Donovan, the lady who invented throwaway diapers. I wonder what babies wore before throwaway diapers? I wonder if Mrs. Davis knows about Mary Anderson and Marion Donovan. If she doesn't, she'll know about them tomorrow!

Mom calls from her room. "Are you and Connie ready for me to quiz you?"

"We're on our way! Be there in a minute," I say.

She calls to me again. "Check the refrigerator. I made us a snack."

Connie and I dash to the fridge door. There's a tray with celery and carrot sticks, ranch dressing, and juice boxes. I grab it and walk toward Mom's room. "After Mom quizzes us, let's take a break and work on the chili for a few minutes. Then we can go back to studying."

Mom's still sitting on the couch with her legs propped on pillows.

"Thanks for the snack tray, Mom."

"Yes, thanks, Mrs. Tibbs. I was getting hungry," says Connie as she takes a carrot stick.

We eat as Mom asks us questions and we give her answers. Connie and I both miss one, so Mom makes us talk about the ones we missed. When she quizzes us the second time, we both go three for three!

"Now that's worth a super-duper hug," says Mom. She hugs me first, and then reaches her arms out for Connie.

"Thanks, Mrs. Tibbs."

I'm so happy that Mom shared her hugs with my best friend. Now I don't have to try and explain to Connie what those hugs feel like anymore.

Mom rubs her belly. "Macey and I are going to take a nap. Mya, will you take the clothes out of the washing machine for me and put them in the dryer?"

"Sure, Mom. Connie and I, we'll get it done."

It doesn't take long to unload the washer, fill the dryer, and start those clothes tumbling dry. I turn to my friend. "Ready to cook?"

She nods. "I'll go wash my hands."

I do the same before getting all of the vegetables in one spot on the counter. I think about how Mom made me chop vegetables with the Kitchen Kids chopper because she said it was safer. She said I could chop the vegetables into the perfect little pieces this way.

While Connie puts the spices in alphabetical order, I chop the vegetables, but it's taking a lot longer than I thought. "I don't think it's a bad idea to have bigger pieces of onion and bell pepper in the pot, do you?"

Connie shrugs. "I don't know. Let's try it."

So instead of chopping the veggies three times, I only chop them once. They're a lot bigger, but it doesn't take nearly as much time as it usually takes Mom to do the same thing. If the chili turns out good, I'll share my chopping secret with her! She'll be so proud.

Once I'm done with that, I dump tomato sauce and a can of diced tomatoes into the bowl, wipe my hands on a dish towel, and smile at Connie.

"I need chili powder, please," I say.

Connie holds up the container. "My name is Charlotte. I live in Chicago. And I make chili powder for a living."

I nod and grin, knowing she's playing the name game that Mom and I play when we make chili. "Well, Charlotte from Chicago, I'm getting ready to turn on the microwave."

"Okay, remember to stir everything a few times first."

"It looks good, Connie." I stuff Mom's recipe back into the coffee can. "Mrs. Frazier is going to have a cow when she realizes two fourth graders beat her."

I poke my head into Mom's room to let her know it's microwave time.

Connie dips a spoon into the bowl for a taste. "Not bad! But we had more bowls of ingredients yesterday, didn't we?"

I set the microwave timer for three minutes and then close the door. "We couldn't have. We had all of our ingredients on the counter, and all of the spices. This pot of chili is going to be good. Let's get back to studying."

It's hard to study knowing I have chili in the microwave. Every three minutes, I stroll to the kitchen, open the microwave door, stir the bowl, and restart the timer. As it gets hotter, I take a good sniff. It smells like chili, and I'm feeling pretty good about it. Mrs. Frazier's face pops into my head. She's going down.

Just as the microwave dings and I take the chili out, Mom waddles into the kitchen. She stirs the chili and smiles. "I could smell it in my room! You and Connie definitely did better than yesterday. You didn't burn anything, but you may want to chop your vegetables smaller next time. Did you use the Kitchen Kids chopper? And where's your chili meat?"

Connie's chair makes a screeching noise as it backs away from the table. "That's it! I knew there was something we were forgetting!"

Firecrackers!

Mom hugs me. "It's okay, Mya, but the judges are very strict about food items that are too big, or too small, or in your case, not in the chili at all, unless you specify you're making vegetarian chili. You've still got a few days before the cook-off to practice. Right now you need to study your Wall of Fame Game questions."

After Connie leaves, I trash the entire bowl of chili. Huge pieces of bell pepper and onion plop to the bottom of the trash bag. I should have taken the time to make small pieces. Why can't I get this right? When Mom and I made chili, it was easy-breezy. We had so much fun, and it didn't seem like it took a long time. Now look at me. I can't even remember to put the right ingredients in the bowl!

Dad and Nugget talk about baseball during dinner. Dad goes on and on about a great catch Nugget made in the outfield. He doesn't mention Nugget's temper tantrum at the ballpark when he threw his bat on the ground. Nugget doesn't mention it either. Actually, my brother doesn't say anything. And that tells me everything.

He struck out again.

I'm really confused now. I thought Nugget tried out for baseball because he wanted to spend time with Dad. Well, Dad's coming to his practices, but Nugget is still mad. There must be something else going on that he hasn't told me. I'd ask him, but I've got my own problems to deal with. I can just see Naomi in her bedroom, with a candle lit, studying her Wall of Fame Game questions. And I bet Mrs. Frazier made ten pots of practice chili today.

"I'm finished eating, so I'm going to study my Wall of Fame Game questions," I say.

Dad nods. "Good plan. What about you, Nugget?"

He scoots back from the table. "I'm going to call Fish."

Nugget and I leave the table as Mom and Dad look at each other and shrug. I put on my pajamas and study a few more hours. Since one of my questions tomorrow is about birds that can't fly, I thought I'd check them out in my book about birds. By ten thirty, my eyes water, and I can't concentrate. I grab my Wall of Fame Questions for tomorrow and lay them on my pillow. Maybe if I keep the questions close to my brain, I won't forget the answers like I forgot to put meat in the chili.

Once my head hits the pillow, my first little mini dream is Naomi Jackson wearing that Wall of Lame loser T-shirt. I grin and roll over. That's a good sign.

Chapter Eighteen

When the alarm buzzes, I hit it with my fist. No way. How can it be Tuesday already when I just closed my eyes a few minutes ago? And what's this stuck on my face? Oh, my Wall of Fame Game questions. I peel them off, toss the paper on my bed, and drag myself to the bathroom. I turn on the light, look in the mirror, and—

AAAAAAGH!!!

My eyes open so wide that my eyeballs almost fall into the sink.

Knock. Knock.

"Mya! What's wrong? Are you okay? Open up!"

I can't let Nugget see my forehead. I can't let anyone see it! "I'm . . . I'm fine, Nugget. I . . . bumped my toe on the door."

"Oh, okay," he says. "Just checking."

When I hear him shuffle back to his room, I dunk my whole face under the faucet, scrub soap across my forehead, and pray everything comes off. It's not coming off! Firecrackers! How can I hide my forehead?

The idea comes so quickly that I rush to finish washing up, brush my teeth, and get dressed. My cowgirl hat covers my forehead just right! And it matches my pink cowgirl boots. What a perfect idea! Yippee-ki-yay! Yes, sirree!

Downstairs, Mom stands with a comb and brush. "How many braids—"

I wave at her and push my hat farther down on my head. "Not this morning, Mom! I've got to go. See you later."

I grab an apple off the table, close the front door, and *ka-clunk* down the street with my brother. He's walking with his head down and his hands stuffed in his pockets. That should give me more time to go over my Wall of Fame Game questions in my head. But first I need to make sure he's okay.

"How's baseball practice going?"

"It's not," he says. "I got to bat twice yesterday, and struck out both times. Dad was there."

I slow my walk, just enough to get up enough nerve to tell my brother about yesterday.

"Connie and I hid behind a tree and watched your practice."

He nods. "I saw you."

I'm happy that he's not mad, but upset that I'm not a better spy. "Oh. Well, I have a question. What did you tell Solo? Whatever it was helped him hit that home run."

Nugget's face brightens as he yanks his hands out of his pockets and pretends to hold a baseball. "It wasn't just Solo. I showed all of my teammates how to watch the spin of the ball. It takes a lot of focus, but if you do it, your chances of getting a hit are good. A breaking ball has a spin on it that looks like—"

I put up a hand. "I don't really care about all that. So, my second question is, if you can tell everybody else how to hit the ball, why do you keep striking out?"

He stuffs his hands back in his pockets. His head drops back down, and I know I asked the golden question.

"If I knew why, then I could fix it and *really* help my team."

I nudge my shoulder into him. "When you figure everything out, you'll be boo-yang good."

The walk to school is a fast one. As soon as I step into the hall, Mr. Winky stops me.

"Good morning, Mya. You sure look like a famous cowgirl this morning. But remember to remove that hat, okie dokie?"

Nokie dokie. "Mr. Winky, I'm . . . uh . . . having a bad hair day. Please don't make me take my hat off. I need to concentrate on making the Wall of Fame, not on my hair."

He smiles. "Sometimes bad hair isn't fair, and it's not that I don't care, but a rule is a rule, especially at this school."

Great. My principal thinks he's Dr. Seuss. "I'll take it off as soon as I get to class," I say. I *ka-clunk* down the hall and into my classroom.

"Good morning, Mya," says Mrs. Davis. "Nice hat, but you'll have to take it off."

"Can I take it off in the cave?"

Mrs. Davis shakes her head. "Now, Mya."

I slowly take off my cowgirl hat and stand in front of my teacher like I have the worst haircut in the history of haircuts. A wrinkle forms above her eyebrows.

"What is that on your forehead, Mya?"

I don't answer her because I know that soon, someone will . . .

Michael yells. "Look! There's an eagle on Mya's forehead!"

My cheeks heat as I stare at the floor while a mob of classmates rush out of the cave and surround me. They giggle, whisper, and point. I keep my eyes on Mrs. Davis, because she looks how I feel; shocked, embarrassed, and wishing the hat had stayed on. Naomi worms her way through the crowd, points at my forehead, and laughs louder than anybody.

Suddenly she stops. "Mrs. Davis, I think Mya is trying to cheat. Does she have a Wall of Fame Game question about birds? I did yesterday."

Mrs. Davis flips pages on her clipboard. *Oh, no!* If I don't say something, Naomi is going to get me disqualified, just like she did for the Fall Festival VIP tickets a few weeks ago. I'm embarrassed enough for having an eagle on my face. Now I have to tell everybody how it got there.

"I fell asleep with the Wall of Fame Game questions on my pillow. When I woke up this morning, the paper was stuck to my face, and I had an eagle on my forehead. I swear that's what happened."

"An eagle on your forehead is good karma, Mya," says Starr.

"It's definitely good karma," says Skye.

"I like eagles," says Connie. "And seriously, how can Mya cheat with a tattoo on her forehead? It's not like she can see it."

Mrs. Davis waves her hand. "I agree, Connie, and besides, an eagle is not the correct answer for any of Mya's questions. All right, class, the bell will ring in a few minutes. If you're not at your seat, I will count you late. Mya, make sure that hat goes in your cabinet."

"Yes, ma'am."

Just as I get to my cabinet in the cave, Naomi gets in my face.

"You definitely belong on the Wall of Lame." She rolls her eyes and heads for the classroom.

Having Naomi Jackson in my head and an eagle on it is a lot for me this morning. I can't think. Everybody's staring at me. What's the question about ostriches?

Good grief. I'm in trouble.

After the bell rings, Mrs. Hansen comes into our room again. I watch a bunch of my classmates, one by one, go into the cave with smiles, and some come out looking like they just sucked a lemon. Mrs. Davis looks my way.

"Mya? You're up."

I follow her like a lost puppy. When we get to the back of the cave, she closes the curtain. "Get your game face on, Mya."

I'm trying, but I feel more like crying.

Mrs. Davis winds the egg timer, and my body feels as if I'm what she's winding.

"Here's your first question: name two fruits that do not grow on trees."

I take a deep breath. "Blueberries and water-melons."

"Good. Name two inventors and their inventions."

"Sure! Mary Anderson, who invented windshield wipers, and Marion Donovan, who invented chili."

Mrs. Davis looks at me. "Did you say chili?"

Good gravy in the navy.

"Throwaway diapers. Isn't that what I said?"

Mrs. Davis shakes her head and then continues. "Name two birds that do not fly."

She's staring at my forehead, but I've got to get over that. "Penguins and ostriches."

Mrs. Davis hits the timer. "Wow! Very well done. You answered all three questions correctly. You are eligible to continue the Wall of Fame Game tomorrow."

I take a deep breath and lift my shoulders as close to my ears as I can. When I let the air out through my nose, I slowly bring my shoulders down. Yeah, I feel so much better.

"Mrs. Davis, you know what's really weird? Ostriches have tiny little brains! They can fit in a teaspoon. That would be T-S-P, not T-B-S-P, if you were using measuring spoons. And they don't really stick their heads in the sand. They're just resting their necks on the ground. I learned that when I looked up my answers. Cool questions."

She smiles like I gave her a million bucks! "I'm so glad you're finding the questions interesting, Mya. You don't know how good that makes me feel as a teacher."

Chapter Nineteen

I'm so glad I'm still in the race. Connie got all her answers right, too! And it's nice knowing that I made Mrs. Davis smile. But I was only being honest. There's a lot of awesome stuff I'm learning just by studying the Wall of Fame Game questions. I'm looking forward to the next ones, just to see what I might learn!

The rest of my afternoon is nothing compared to the morning. Everything flies, except that eagle on my forehead. Connie says it will stay on my forehead for a few days until the ink wears off.

Good gravy.

It's almost time to go home, and when Mrs. Davis stands with a stack of papers, it's not hard to guess what she's got.

WALL OF FAME GAME QUESTIONS FOR MYA TIBBS:

WEDNESDAY

1. Name three Civil War battles.
2. Name three countries that border the Pacific Ocean.
3. Name three sports played at the Summer Olympics.

Mrs. Davis has turned up the heat. I'm in trouble. I can't think of an answer for any of the questions, and I have to come up with three for each one! When the bell rings, I stay in my seat, stuck in scared. Connie comes over to my desk.

"Come on, let's get our stuff and leave."

I sit on a bench in the cave, still wondering if the questions tomorrow are going to take me down. I can't let Naomi beat me. There's no way I can wear that T-shirt. And cowgirls are not dumb! I take another look at my questions and wonder if any cowgirl in the history of cowgirl nation ever had to answer these.

Connie and I are the last ones to leave the cave. On our way out, we say good-bye to Mrs. Davis, and I notice Kenyan standing in front of the Wall of Fame. I don't usually talk to Kenyan because last year in third grade, he pulled my braids. But he's standing there all alone, just staring at the wall. I walk over to him.

"Hi."

"Hey," says Kenyan.

"Are you still in the game?" I ask.

"I'm still in it. Are you?"

"Yeah," I say. "Why are you just standing here?"

"I'll tell you if you promise to keep it a secret."

Holy moly. I wasn't expecting him to say that. But by the look on his face, he really wants to tell me something.

"I promise."

Kenyan points to a spot a few columns from the beginning. "See that name, Kenyan Tayler? That's my uncle. I was named after him. He made the wall. Isn't that cool? He told me it was the hardest thing he did in the fourth grade, but he's not very proud of himself."

It takes me a while to find his uncle because I've

never looked at that row of names before. When I find him, I shrug. "Why is he not proud? Making the Wall of Fame is a big deal," I say.

Kenyan lowers his head and stares at the floor. "He cheated. The only person who knows is me, and now you. He's ashamed, and keeps telling me he's sorry. I think if I can make the wall, one no-cheating Kenyan will erase the cheating of the other Kenyan. Then we can both be happy. He's been helping me study."

"That's a lot of pressure on you. And anyway, everybody has different questions. How could he cheat?"

"Everybody had the same questions when he was in this class."

I nod. "That's boo-yang cool of you to do that for your uncle, Kenyan. I think . . ."

I stare at two names not far from Kenyan's uncle—names I had never noticed before.

"I think . . ."

"Mya, are you okay?" Kenyan asks.

I keep staring. It can't be!

Kenyan touches my shoulder. "Mya, can you hear me?"

This is a bad surprise, a really bad one.

He shakes my backpack. "Mya, can you hear me?

Do you want me to get Mrs. Davis?"

I shake my head, but my eyes stay glued to the wall. I can't believe what I'm reading.

Darrell Tibbs
Monica James

Mom's last name was James before she got married. There they are, right next to each other on the wall. And they didn't even tell me.

I've got to get out of here. Where's the door? I run as fast as I can.

"Mya, stop running," says Mrs. Davis.

I can't.

I'm trying to get as far away from that wall as I can. I dash down the hall, push open the front door of my school, and call to the one person I need right now.

"Connie!"

The look on my face must match how I'm feeling, because she runs toward me.

"What happened? Did Kenyan say something that wasn't nice? Where is he?"

I'm out of breath, shaking my head, trying to explain. "The wall! They didn't even tell me. How was I supposed to know?"

"Slow down, Mya! What are you talking about?"

A voice I recognize answers for me.

"She found them," says Nugget. "Our parents are on the wall."

Fish is with him. "Well, that's awesome . . . isn't it?"

I wipe my eyes. "They didn't tell me. Why didn't you tell me, Nugget?"

"Because they asked me not to. They didn't tell me either, when I was in fourth grade. You can't let them know you found out, Mya. They'll think I told you."

I shrug. "Why would they keep that a secret?"

And then it all makes sense to me.

"Dad told me at Open House that Mom said I didn't have to sign up for the Wall of Fame Game if I didn't want to. I bet she doesn't think I could do it."

Connie shakes her head. "Wait, Mya, that doesn't sound like—"

Nugget interrupts Connie and nods at me. "Kind of like how Dad doesn't think I can play baseball. Look, I'm going to practice now. After dinner tonight, we need to ask Mom and Dad what's going on."

I try not to cry. "That's why they're so into Macey. They think she's going to be smarter than me and play baseball better than Nugget."

"That can't be true, Mya Papaya. I think you and Nugget need to talk to your parents," says Fish.

"Me, too," says Connie. "I'm pretty sure you've got things wrong, Mya. Your mom is way too nice to believe something like that. You still want me to come over?"

I nod, because I can't do anything else.

Fish and Nugget leave for baseball practice while Connie and I walk to my house. My Wednesday Wall of Fame Game questions feel like a brick in my backpack, even though I'm sure they don't weigh more than Monday's or Tuesday's. Maybe it's because they need more answers.

I keep *ka-clunk*ing. "I'm all mixed up, Connie. Why didn't they tell me? Why wouldn't they tell Nugget? I'm going to have to study forever. And we still haven't gotten the chili right."

Connie shrugs. "We've got to come up with nine answers tomorrow, and twelve on Thursday. I don't even want to think about Friday. Maybe we should drop out of the cook-off. That's just my opinion."

I shake my head. "No way! I have so much I need to prove to Mom."

My body tightens as I walk. My toes curl inside my boots, and it hurts as I walk. I take a big breath and let it out, hoping it will make me relax. But the moment I let out that big breath of air, I picture myself standing with Kenyan, listening to him tell me about his cheating uncle. And then, before I can say anything—*boom!* I find my parents on the wall.

My mind switches to show me Naomi at home, studying her questions, and probably eating cake and ice cream, too.

Worst of all, I picture Mom, holding Macey, telling her, "Your sister couldn't make the wall, and she can't make chili, either."

Chapter Twenty

I grab my friend's arm before we go in my house. "It's too much, Connie. I can't handle all these problems by myself. You won't quit on me, right? We'll keep studying together, and you're going to help me with the chili, aren't you?"

Connie puts her arm around my neck. "I won't quit on you, Mya. I'm just worried about having enough time to study. I've got a big reason for making the wall, too. Just like you. It doesn't have anything to do with me. But it's important."

I haven't thought about Connie's reasons for wanting to make the Wall of Fame. She hasn't really talked about it. I wonder if it's a secret, like Kenyan's? I'll ask her later.

Mom's on the sofa folding some of the clothes she got for Macey at the baby shower. I stare at her, wondering what she's thinking about, because I'm sure it's not me. First she doesn't come to Open House. Then she's not upset about us missing the Annie Oakley marathon. She tried to cancel the chili cook-off, and now I find out that maybe she thinks I'm not smart.

Mom smiles our way. "Hey there! I can't wait to dress Macey in some of these outfits. She's going to look adorable."

I head toward the stairs without looking at her. "I wish I could help you, but I've got a bunch of questions that I have to answer tomorrow for the Wall of Fame Game. And somehow Connie and I have to figure out how to make a good pot of chili between studying."

Mom calls out. "Mya, I want you to take a rest from the kitchen today. Use that extra time to study your questions. That's more important."

I spin around, totally shocked, and ready to cry. "But Mom!"

"No buts. And once you get those answers down, bring me your question sheet so I can quiz you."

I squeeze the straps of my backpack and head upstairs. Connie follows me. As soon as I get to my room, I fling my backpack on the bed. "What am I supposed to do now?"

"How about study?" says Connie. She takes her Monday and Tuesday questions out of her backpack and begins to draw on them.

"You tell me to study, and you're drawing pictures on old Wall of Fame Game question sheets? Why would you even keep those? I trashed mine."

She colors the edges of the sheets with crayons. "I give them to Clayton. He likes them."

I *ka-clunk* from one end of my room to the other. "Maybe I'll give mine to Naomi, so she'll have something colorful to remind her of how I whipped her in the Wall of Fame Game. I can't lose that bet, Connie. But, you know, Mom has got to let me practice my chili makin'. How in the world am I supposed to beat Mrs. Frazier if I can't go in the kitchen?"

She looks up at me. "I agree with your mom, Mya."

I stop walking. "What?"

I haven't seen Connie's face so angry since Mrs. Davis made us be Spirit Week partners, and that makes me nervous.

"I'm so tired of hearing you talk about beating

Naomi and beating Mrs. Frazier. Is that all you know? And if I found out my parents were on the wall, the very last thing I would think is that they're against me. You've got the nicest parents in Bluebonnet. You're going to feel so bad when you find out the truth."

I put my hands on my hips. "Well, excuse me, Connie Tate, but I think I know my parents better than you do!"

"Your mom even helped us study! What's wrong with you, Mya? Never mind. I'm leaving."

"Wait, Connie. You're tired of hearing me talk about why I'm doing the Wall of Fame Game, but what makes you think your reasons are better than mine? You didn't even bother to tell me why you want to make the wall."

She's almost screaming at me. "I told you at Open House, but your head is so full of beating Naomi that you totally forgot! I've got a really good reason. If I make the wall, I'll be the first person in my family to do it. Both my parents went to Young Elementary, but they missed questions, right at the end of the game. They haven't said anything to me about it, but I know they're hoping I make it. And I want to do it for myself, and my little brother, Clayton."

All those names on the wall, and none of them

are Tate. Holy moly. Connie grabs the pictures she was coloring and stuffs them back in her backpack.

"I want Clayton to know he can do it. Your whole family is on the wall. You should be happy. You're smart, Mya, and making the Wall of Fame shouldn't be about Naomi Jackson."

I frown at her. "Why not? I'm not wearin' that stinkin' T-shirt."

Connie grabs her backpack. "I wish I had never made that T-shirt! Remember what F.A.M.E. means? It's not about proving you're smarter than somebody else. The letters mean 'For All My Efforts.' So if somebody asked, 'Mya, why did you play the Wall of Fame Game?' Your answer will be 'I got on the Wall of Fame just to beat Naomi Jackson.' Seriously, Mya? You gave up Annie Oakley, hanging out with your mom, playing outside, riding your bike, watching television, going to the park after school . . . all for Naomi?"

I frown. "Everybody has a reason for getting on the wall. Mine just happens to be different than yours."

She frowns back. "But don't you think you need to figure out the difference between doing something for a good reason and doing something for a bad one?"

Silence.

Just before she steps into the hallway, Connie turns to me. "Clayton even loves the papers I bring home that I don't need or want anymore. You call it trash. I color on them and give them to my little brother. He tapes them to his wall. I'm already on *his* Wall of Fame."

She disappears from my doorway. I don't know what's going on with Connie, but if I have to stand alone against Naomi and Mrs. Frazier, I will. I've only got a few more days before it will all be over anyway. Until then, I'll do things my way.

Maybe that's what I should've done all along.

I *ka-clunk* over to my bed, unzip my backpack, and snatch out my questions. Question number one. Name three Civil War battles. Three? I thought there was only one!

I get on the internet and find out there's a bunch of Civil War battles! I thought it all happened in one place. I can't help but read about some of them. Let's see, there was a battle in Galveston, and then there's the battle at Liberty. Holy moly! There was even a battle at a place called Cheat Mountain!

I stop reading and think of Kenyan and his uncle. I understand why he wants to make the Wall of Fame. It's a good reason. I tried to tell Connie that everybody has different reasons, but she doesn't want to listen to me.

I'm not cheating. I think about Mom and Macey. They don't know that I've got this bet going on with Naomi. And I'm not even sure Mom thinks I can make the wall. I can always just tell Macey I did this for her, can't I? Okay, maybe that would be cheating.

The words "For All My Efforts" are all I can think of. What am I getting for all my efforts? I'm getting on the wall. Isn't that good enough? Why should the reason I'm doing it matter? Anyway, what's next? Three countries that border the Pacific Ocean. That's easy. United States, Japan, and um . . . Chile.

Good gravy. It doesn't matter that the country is spelled differently. It still reminds me that I've got chili to make, and Mom won't let me in the kitchen today.

I sit on the edge of my bed. Why did I have to remember Chile? I know why. Because that bad-talking lady named Mrs. Frazier is trying to take my mom's title, and I'm not having it! I've got to figure out a way to get in that kitchen and practice.

What's the next question? Three sports in the Summer Olympics. That's easy.

Knock, knock.

Nugget's standing at my door with dirt all over his uniform.

"I hit the ball today! Oh my gosh, Mya, it felt boo-yang good! I just wish I knew what I did to get that hit. I hope it wasn't an accident. Well, at least I hit it, right?"

I nod. "Right! Did you tell any more guys how to hit the ball?"

"I showed two of my teammates what a slider looks like coming out of the pitcher's hand. Once they caught on, they started killin' the ball. Our team is actually looking pretty good."

"Did Dad show up to your practice today?"

"No. I don't care. I hit the ball, so it doesn't matter that he never showed me how."

Mom yells from downstairs. "It's time for dinner. Nugget, take that dirty uniform off before you come to the table."

I grin at him. "Congratulations on getting a hit."

He shoves me on the shoulder. I shove him back.

Mom's got baked chicken, mashed potatoes, and peas on the table, and as soon as Nugget takes a seat, Dad says the blessing. Once he's done, he turns to Nugget.

"I'm sorry I didn't make your practice today. We got busy at the store."

My brother shrugs and shoves a spoonful of peas in his mouth. Dad looks over at Mom before turning to me.

"How was your day, Mya?" asks Dad.

I want to scream that I have to beat Naomi Jackson at the Wall of Fame Game, and Kenyan's uncle cheated, and I got in an argument with Connie, and Mom doesn't want to do anything with me anymore, and she thinks I'm not smart enough to make the Wall of Fame, and she won't let me practice making chili so I might not beat Mrs. Frazier.

But instead I smile. "It was okay."

The dining room is so quiet that I expect to hear crickets rubbing their wings together. I look at the ceiling fan above the table, the picture on the wall, the food on my plate, even the design on the tablecloth. I'm looking at everything just to avoid looking at my parents. I can feel Mom and Dad staring at me.

Suddenly Dad drops his fork on his plate. The sound makes Mom moan.

"I'm sorry, honey," says Dad. "I didn't mean to scare you."

Mom rubs her belly. "I think you scared Macey. She's kicking again."

Dad shakes his head. "She's not kicking. She's

pitching. I think that girl wants to play baseball. As soon as she's old enough, I'll take her in the back-yard and—"

Nugget bangs his fist on the table. He's staring at his food, and there's more steam coming off him than from his mashed potatoes. But it's not nearly as hot at the table as it's about to get, because I think everybody's ready to explode.

Chapter Twenty-One

Dad crosses his arms over his chest as he glares at my brother. "You have something you need to say, Nugget?"

My brother looks up from his plate. His face has all kinds of anger in it. I don't know if I should eat, excuse myself from the table, or just be quiet. I choose the last one as I listen to him go off.

"I can't believe how excited you are about teaching Macey how to catch and hit the ball! I guess I wasn't good enough."

Dad moves his face closer to Nugget's. "What are you talking about, son?"

My brother's voice gets louder. "Every guy on my team got lessons from their dad on how to catch and hit. Every guy except me. At Open House, you didn't even ask me if I wanted to play baseball. You just told all the dads, in front of my friends, that I'm probably more interested in Whiz Kid Camp. Who told you that?"

Nugget's eyes water, and he swipes away the tears with the back of his hand. "You made me look soft in front of the guys. Why'd you do that? Why didn't you teach me how to play, Dad?"

Dad and Nugget have a stare down that lasts only a few seconds. Both my knees are jumping like crazy under the table. Suddenly Dad breaks his stare-off with Nugget and glares at me.

"I'll be right back. Don't move."

Moments later, he returns, and puts his fist on the table. Slowly, his fingers open like a flower bud when it blooms. Inside his hand are two little white things.

"Are those animal bones?" asks Nugget.

He reaches for them, but Dad closes his hand back to a fist.

"I've had these bird bones since I was eight years old. Found them. I took 'em to school every day, and after school, my science teacher let me look at them under the microscope until it was time to go home. I kept a journal on what I saw. I wanted to figure out how that bird died."

"What does that have to do with baseball?" asks Nugget.

Dad shrugs. "For me, everything. But let me finish my story. Later that year, my father decided I should try out for baseball. I didn't like it, but he made me catch twenty-five fly balls every day, and if I missed one, I had to start all over. And then I had to hit a ball off a tee."

"At least he taught you how to play," says Nugget. "That's more than you did for me."

Dad waits before he finishes. "All I wanted to do was read science magazines and look at stuff under a microscope. I wanted my dad to like science and look at stuff under the microscope with me. I asked for a science set for Christmas. I got a glove and a bat."

The table's quiet. Nugget's eyes are glued on Dad's as he keeps talking. "My dad made me play, and I swore, when I got old enough to make my own decisions, I'd quit. But I ended up being good at baseball. I still wanted to quit when I was in high school, but I knew I'd be letting my team down. And then I got a college scholarship. Dad thinks he did me a favor. Maybe he did, maybe he didn't."

I slowly take a look at Mom. Her eyebrows rise as she looks back at me. I turn back and listen to Dad.

"So years later, I get married, have a son, and when he's old enough to play baseball I buy him a glove and a bat. We go out in the yard, and he has trouble catching the ball, but he sees a butterfly, chases it, and asks me, 'Do all caterpillars turn into butterflies?' I thought that was an incredible question for a six-year-old boy, but instead of talking to you about caterpillars, I talked to you about curveballs, sliders, knuckleballs, and change-ups. To me, we were out there to play baseball, not talk science. That's what my dad taught me."

Mom interrupts. "The next day, I looked out the window and saw you and your dad staring at a worm that you had in your hand. Both baseball gloves were in the grass, and so was the bat."

Dad looks right at my brother. "I realized, at that moment, while you held that wiggly worm in your hand, that you weren't interested in baseball. Your mind was beyond baseball. And if I wasn't careful, I would do to you what my dad did to me. So I stopped asking you to play ball, and we bought you a microscope, which you loved from the moment I gave it to you. I started asking you what *you* wanted to do. You said you wanted to visit the science store. I would have given anything for my dad to have asked me that question."

"I love that place. I love my microscope, too," says Nugget.

"So do I!" says Dad. "The only person who really knew that I was more nerd than athlete was your mother. I'm never going to force you to be anything but yourself. I don't want you trying to play baseball just because I played. Nobody knows how much I hated playing that game."

"And that's why you didn't show me how to play baseball?" asks Nugget.

"No. You weren't interested, and I wasn't going to force you. But I'm amazed at how you've remembered all the pitches I showed you," says Dad. He looks my way.

"Do you have something you need to talk about, Mya?"

I swallow, even though I don't have anything in my mouth. "Today Kenyan showed me his uncle's name on the Wall of Fame."

Mom coughs. I turn to help her and notice she's eyeballing Dad, and he's staring back at her. Very softly she asks me, "Is Kenyan's last name Tayler?"

I nod. "I saw your and Dad's names right next to

Kenyan's uncle. Why didn't you tell me you were on the wall? Why did you keep it a secret? When I saw your names today, the first thing I thought was that you didn't think I could make the wall, and that's why you didn't tell me."

Mom holds up her hand. "Darrell, I've got this one."

She turns to me. "We didn't want to pressure you. If we had told you that we were on the wall, you might have felt obligated to sign up. That's not what the wall is about."

"Oh" is all I can say. I wonder if she can see the "I'm sorry" in my eyes. I'm scared to open my mouth because I might just cry for being so silly. How did I let myself think Mom would ever do something to hurt me?

"Mya, Nugget, come here," says Dad.

We scoot back from our seats and stand in front of our father. He takes our hands.

"Whatever you choose to do in life, it should be something you are passionate about, something you want to do—not because you tried to follow in someone else's footsteps. And that includes ours. Your mother and I love you, and think you're perfect, just the way you are."

"Okay," says Nugget. "I thought you believed I was a loser, and that's why you pushed me behind you at Open House."

Dad shakes his head. "Just the opposite. I was protecting you from that mob of sports dads because I believe you're a winner and will one day do something to change the world for the better."

Nugget stares at his shoes. "Yes, sir. That's what I'm going to do. So can I have a look at the bird bones now?"

"Let's go check 'em out under your microscope," says Dad.

As Nugget and Dad leave the dining room, I glance over at Mom.

"Nerds are awesome," she says.

I giggle. "Yeah. They are."

"But I'm glad they're gone so I can have a little time alone with my number one daughter."

Connie's right. I *do* have the best parents in Bluebonnet.

"Go get your Wall of Fame Game questions, Mya. Let's go over them."

I rush upstairs and bring them to the table. She starts right away.

"Name three Civil War battles."

"Um, let's see. There's Cheat Mountain, Liberty, and . . . uh . . . what's the third one? I can't remember, Mom."

She looks at me. "Galveston is the one you wrote down. Name three countries that border the Pacific Ocean."

I close my eyes. "The United States for sure. And Chile, and . . . oh, Japan."

Mom gives me another look. "You have to get these down, Mya. Last question. Name three sports in the Summer Olympics."

"Basketball, track and field, and equestrian."

She smiles. "I want you to go upstairs and study. The questions are going to get harder, and you have to get these right to move on to the next round."

"Yes, ma'am."

I go upstairs and read the questions and answers over and over again, but I'm worried about tomorrow. Two misses and I'm out. I can't lose to Naomi. I just can't.

Chapter Twenty-Two

Wednesday morning, I practice my Wall of Fame Game answers as I put on my clothes. I ask Annie Oakley and Cowgirl Claire questions, and then answer them when they don't. Mom gives me nine thick braids, one for each of today's Wall of Fame Game answers.

On the way to school, I give Nugget my questions, and he quizzes me one last time. When we're done, we fist-bump, and then he nudges me.

"You got them all right, genius."

I can't believe he called me genius, especially

when there's a good chance that he really is one. "Thanks, Nugget. I just hope I don't get everything all jumbled."

"You won't. See you at lunch."

In class, I try to keep my answers at the front of my brain as I watch Mrs. Davis call my classmates from the rows before mine. She hasn't called many names. I guess there's not many of us left.

"Mya, you're up," says Mrs. Davis.

I slide out of my seat. "Okay."

Once we get to the back of the cave, and Mrs. Davis closes the curtains, I give her my game face without her asking for it.

"Mrs. Davis, before you hit the timer, can I tell you something?"

"Sure, Mya, what's on your mind?"

I sit down beside her. "There's some interesting stuff in these questions. Have you ever read the story of the Civil War? You should check it out! And if you think about how big the countries are that border the Pacific, you have to wonder, how big is that ocean? I looked it up. Did you know it's not only the biggest ocean, it's the deepest one, too! Holy moly!"

Mrs. Davis smiles. "Isn't that something?"

"Yes!" I say, laughing. "But anyway, I'm ready now."

She hits the egg timer. "Good! Okay, here we go. Name three Civil War battles."

I tell her the answers without thinking about it. "Liberty, Cheat Mountain, and Galveston."

"Good," says Mrs. Davis. "Name three countries that border the Pacific Ocean."

"The United States for sure, Japan, and . . . Japan, and . . ."

"Relax, Mya."

My heart's beating so loudly that I can't hear my brain give me the answer. I can't remember! "Mrs. Davis, please repeat the question."

"Name three countries that border the Pacific Ocean."

This happened to David on Monday. He froze. Now I'm going to do the same thing. And tonight, when I practice making chili . . .

Wait . . .

"Chile, Mrs. Davis! United States, Japan, and Chile!"

"Correct! Name three sports in the Summer Olympics. Hurry, Mya."

"Track and field, basketball, and equestrian,

which is a fancy word for rodeo riding with a horse that's got manners."

Ding.

I sit beside her and wipe my forehead, both of us breathing like we just ran a race.

"I don't know if I'm more proud of you for getting the answers right, or for not giving up. I thought Nugget was good last year, but that was flat-out amazing. Now I'm wondering how good your baby sister is going to be. What's her name?"

"Macey."

Mrs. Davis shakes her head. "You're going to be a great example for her, like Nugget was for you. Congratulations, Mya. You answered all the questions correctly, which means you're still eligible for tomorrow's Wall of Fame Game questions."

"Thank you, Mrs. Davis," I say. Then I turn around and leave the cave.

As I enter the classroom, all eyes are on me. I look to my best friend and smile. She smiles back. I've never been so happy to see her smile as I am right now. But I get just as nervous the moment Mrs. Davis calls Connie's name. I watch them head to the back of the cave. I close my eyes and whisper. "Come on, Connie, you can do it."

When she comes back wearing a big smile, I tap my foot as if I can hear music.

There's lots of talk in the cafeteria and on the playground about who's left and who's out in the Wall of Fame Game. I walk with Connie, even though we're not talking that much. Finally I take a deep breath and tell her what's on my mind.

"Connie, I'm sorry for being so mean to you. You are right about me having awesome parents, and I've been thinking about everything you said to me yesterday when you were in my room. I thought you were doing the Wall of Fame Game to get your parents to notice you. That's what you said at Open House."

"And I meant it. I'll be the first Tate on the Wall of Fame, and they'll be very happy about it. So will I. But I'm mostly doing it for my little brother, so that when he gets to fourth grade, he'll see my name and know that he can make the wall, too."

I nod. "Yeah, that's a really good reason for getting on the wall."

"What about your reason, Mya? You still think it's a good one?" asks Connie.

"Well, like I said, after you left yesterday, I did a lot of thinking. And I realized beating Naomi is not a good reason to make the wall. But I can't go back on the bet."

"Naomi doesn't have to know your reasons. You're the only person who knows mine."

I smile at my best friend. "And Clayton is a good reason."

She smiles back. "Macey would be, too."

"Yeah, she would be," I say.

We spot Nugget kicking a soccer ball to Fish, so we tell them that we made it through to the next round.

Nugget gives us high fives. "Why didn't you tell me at lunch?"

"I think I was still nervous," I say.

He nods. "That's boo-yang cool! You're almost there, but Thursday and Friday are back-breaker days, the absolute worst. If you can make it through Thursday, you've got a good shot."

Connie sweeps loose hair behind her ear. "Is Thursday really *that* bad?"

Fish turns around and walks backward as he talks to us. "On Thursday, it won't feel like a game anymore. It's a war worse than any battle you've ever been in. If you're still in it on Thursday, it's because you've got a shot at making the wall, and Mrs. Davis is going to make you earn it."

Connie nods. "Makes a lot of sense. Thanks for the tip, guys."

As Fish and my brother run toward the soccer goals, I feel volcano lava in my belly again.

"I don't want to picture Naomi in my mind while I study anymore," I say.

Connie smiles. "That's good news. So do you want me to come over your house today, Mya?"

As much as I want to tell her yes, I've got lots of thinking to do, and some of it has nothing to do with the questions.

"I think you need to let Clayton play in your room while you study tonight. He's the reason you're doing the Wall of Fame Game, right?"

Connie nods. "Have you changed your reasons for getting on the wall?"

All I can do is shrug. A few days ago, my reason was as sure as Annie Oakley catching the bad guys in her movies.

Mrs. Davis blows the whistle, and we all rush to line up. I think about Connie's question for the rest of the afternoon, until Mrs. Davis hands out Thursday's Wall of Fame Game questions. There's three questions as usual, except each question needs four answers.

I close my eyes. Fish is right.

This is going to be war.

WALL OF FAME GAME QUESTIONS FOR MYA
TIBBS:

THURSDAY

1. Name four of the thirteen original American
   colonies.

2. Name the four stages of the water cycle.

3. Name four major organs in the human body.

Chapter Twenty-Three

Fish and Nugget are at it again on the way home, but this time, it's much more serious.

"Don't quit the team, Nugget," says Fish.

"I don't have any reason to stay now. It's over. I'll tell Mr. Booker tomorrow in class."

We're at the crosswalk, waiting for the sign to change. Fish's face is redder than strawberries. The *Don't Walk* changes to *Walk*. Nugget, Connie, and I cross the street.

Fish yells to Nugget from the sidewalk, "I thought you got everything straightened out last night with your dad. Don't quit now!"

My brother keeps walking toward home. Soon Connie turns toward her apartment complex. I want to say something to my brother, but I just don't know what would be good.

Once he opens the door, Nugget goes straight to his room. I go to mine, drop my backpack on my bed, and then go look for Mom. She's in Macey's room, rocking in the chair.

"Hey, Mom. Are you okay?"

She grins and rubs her stomach. "I'm better than okay, Mya. It won't be long before Macey's here. I feel her moving around, but it's a different kind of moving than normal."

I sit on the floor at Mom's feet. Her ankles are still swollen, but she's smiling.

Suddenly, I recognize the music playing. "Mom, is that my old *Rappin' Rhymes Before Nappin' Times* CD?"

She giggles. "It sure is. You can't find that CD anymore. You kids download everything nowadays. But I saved this one. You and Nugget both loved it, and I hope Macey does, too."

The room is filled with hand-me-downs from Nugget and me. Each thing I look at brings back a memory. There's a stack of books in the corner, a little wooden chair, and a box of toys.

I tap my fingers on the carpet to the nursery rhyme music and sit quietly near Mom as I think about my talk with Connie at recess. She's being an awesome big sister for Clayton. Maybe it's time I step up and be one for Macey.

"I wanted to work on this room today, but I just didn't feel up to it," she says. "I thought if I came in here and sat down, it would motivate me, but it hasn't. I'm going to go soak my ankles in the tub."

"Don't worry, Mom. We'll get Macey's room finished. Remember, we do things for each other. That's the Tibbs way, right?"

She keeps grinning. "Macey's lucky to have a big sister like you, Mya. So lucky. How'd the Wall of Fame Game go today?"

"Three for three, but it was so hard! I almost missed one. I've been thinking about the chili cook-off, too. Can I try to make a quick batch before I start studying?"

Mom shakes her head. "A quick batch? No such thing. Do you remember our talk about chili last Saturday, when you told me you signed us up for the cook-off?"

I nod, and she keeps talking. "I told you that some things should not be changed. So while you're working on your Wall of Fame Game questions, you think some more on that. And I know you're not going to like this, but I want you to take another day off from working in the kitchen. You've got a lot going on, Mya, with the Wall of Fame Game and this cook-off. Sometimes you need to just sit, be quiet, and think."

I stand and try to explain. "I don't have time to just sit, be quiet, and think! And if I can't practice making chili today, I might as well quit the cook-off!"

She stops rocking. "Why are you talking about quitting? We're not quitters! And if you don't have time to sit and think, how will you find time to make perfect chili? There's more to making good food than what's on the recipe. Now go work on your questions before dinner."

"Yes, ma'am."

I have no idea what I said wrong. Maybe I do need to sit and think. That's what I was doing when I realized Connie was right about good and bad reasons to make the wall. That's what I'll do. I'll slow down for a minute and take some time to figure out why Mom won't let me go back in the kitchen.

Upstairs, I notice my brother's door isn't all the way closed. I knock on it, and he lets me in, then falls back on his bed. He's playing a game on his phone and doesn't look at me. I stand near the door.

"Can I tell you something that Connie told me?"

He keeps playing his game. "It's a free country. Say whatever you want."

I walk over to his window and look out. "I think I may have done something right, but I did it for the wrong reason."

Silence.

"I didn't tell you about this, and only Connie— well, and everybody in my class—knows. I signed up for the Wall of Fame Game just to win a bet against Naomi Jackson. She said cowgirls weren't as smart as beauty pageant winners. I wanted her to eat those words."

Nugget drops his cell on the bed. He sits up and frowns at me. "Have you lost your mind? The Wall of Fame Game is about honor, and pride, and it's For All My Efforts, remember? You don't even like Naomi Jackson! I can't believe you would sign up for the Wall of Fame Game just to beat her."

I keep staring out the window because I don't want to look at him. His voice has so much angry in it that I'm scared to turn around. He keeps talking.

"Mom and Dad would flip out if they knew you took a bet for the Wall of Fame Game."

I've heard enough, so I grab my backpack and stand in his doorway. "You should look in the mirror, Nugget. Don't you get it? I'm doing the Wall of Fame Game for the wrong reason. I was only doing it to prove something to Naomi. You tried out for baseball for the wrong reason. You only did it to prove something to Dad. And that's bad because you really love baseball, and you know so much about it. The difference is, you're going to quit. Naomi Jackson can't make me quit. I've found the right reason to make the wall, and it has nothing to do with Naomi. You need to find the right reason for playing baseball without giving up."

I *ka-clunk* out of his room. Nugget needed a kick in the pants, and I gave it to him.

He's a Tibbs. And so am I. We're not quitters. *Thanks, Mom, for reminding me of that.*

I sit in my room for a long time, thinking about what I said to Nugget, and how I thought just like him only a few days ago. I had stinkin' thinkin', but I figured it out. Naomi is not going to be my reason for making the Wall of Fame. Now if I can just figure out what I'm doing wrong with the chili.

After sitting in my room for almost thirty minutes, I grab my backpack and head to Macey's room.

As soon as I walk in, I feel better. Mom's gone to take her nap. It's so calm in here, and the *Rappin' Rhymes for Nappin' Times* music makes me giggle. I unzip my backpack and take out my questions. Just looking at them makes my heart thump.

1. Name four of the thirteen original American colonies.
2. Name the four stages of the water cycle.
3. Name four major organs in the human body.

I think about what happened today and then picture myself standing in the cave with Mrs. Davis. She's asking me questions about the thirteen colonies and body organs and the water cycle. I'm staring at her like she's speaking a foreign language. Then she tells me I'm disqualified.

I tug on my braids to make me focus and then look at my questions. Name four of the thirteen colonies. Rhode Island, Connecticut, Massachusetts, and . . . firecrackers! What is the answer? I glance at my study sheet. I forgot Georgia, New York, New Jersey. I'll just pick one—Georgia will be my fourth colony.

Georgia, Georgia, Georgia. I say it over and

over until I know it's in there with the other three that I remembered. Next question. Four stages of the water cycle. Okay, there's evaporation, precipitation, condensation, or wait . . . that doesn't sound right. Is that the right order? Firecrackers! This is too hard!

"Mya, why are you studying in Macey's room? Wait a minute . . . is that *Rappin' Rhymes Before Nappin' Times* I hear? No way! I used to rock that music when I was four years old, until I went to sleep." Nugget strolls in, and I frown at him.

"Do you need something? I'm trying to study."

He leans against Macey's crib. "Connie's right. She's really smart."

I put my hands on my hips. "I'm busy, Nugget."

"No. Let me finish. I heard what you said to me. I love baseball. It's my favorite sport. I probably know more about baseball than I do about anything I learn at school. But I'm not good at playing it. I try, but I just can't seem to hit that ball!"

I put down my questions. I can tell when my brother needs me, and right now, he does. I walk over to him. "I know what you mean. I brought home a folder full of A+ papers. Now I've got this Wall of Fame Game, and it shouldn't be that hard, but it is.

I even know which questions are coming, and I still might not get them right."

Nugget stands in front of me. "What did you say about knowing what's coming?"

I roll my eyes. "Even though I know what's coming, I still might not get the answer right. Is that what you're talking about?"

My brother nods. "Yeah. That's what I thought you said. Thanks, Mya."

I shrug. "For what?"

"I think you just helped me figure something out."

I *ka-clunk* back to my spot and take a seat. "Well, good. I wish there was a way you could help me. I need to study now, later, and even while I sleep. I'm really scared that I'm going to get disqualified tomorrow, Nugget. These questions are really hard."

He stares at the ceiling. "There's actually research on learning while you sleep. Look it up on the internet."

"I don't have time! If you know about it, please help me."

"Okay. I'll go look it up. Stay here."

I keep studying, hoping my brother's right. If I can learn while I'm asleep, that will double my study time and give me a better chance at going three for three tomorrow.

A half hour later, Nugget returns with his phone. "I don't know if this is going to work, but we can try, okay? I downloaded a recording app on my phone. Now we can record the questions, and the answers, to play over and over again."

I breathe in and breathe out. "You don't have any idea how much you've helped me."

I shove my brother on the shoulder. He shoves me back and walks over to Macey's crib. I hear him saying the question, and then giving the answer right behind it! If this works, I'm as good as on that Wall of Fame.

Soon Nugget's finished. "I'll set it up for you before we go to bed. We'll know tomorrow if it worked."

"It has to work, Nugget, or else I'm out of the game."

"Keep studying, as if you didn't have the recording. Then when you go to sleep, it will just be repeating what you already know."

"Thanks for helping me."

"You helped me first," he says.

As my brother leaves the room, I believe things will get better for him. But not for me. This is the second day in a row that I haven't practiced making chili, and if I don't learn as I sleep with this recording, I'll lose my chance to make the wall. I didn't think it would mean that much to me since I don't care about my bet with Naomi. But as I stare at Macey's crib, I realize that I want my name on that wall more than I ever did before.

Chapter Twenty-Four

Thursday morning, I feel ten times smarter than I did before I went to bed. I think my head is bigger, filled with perfect answers to my Wall of Fame Game questions! I stand in the mirror like I'm the smartest cowgirl in the country. "I'm the Magnificent Mya Tibbs! I'm going three out of three again today!"

I dress quickly, eat even quicker, and almost run to school. As I step into the cave, there's a rhythm in my *ka-clunk* that I haven't had since Monday.

"Twelve answers for three questions," says Starr.

"Twelve for three," says Starr.

"That's just ridiculous," says Starr.

"Totally ridiculous," says Skye.

Starr hugs me. "You're going to do it, Mya. We can feel it."

Skye hugs me, too. "We definitely feel it."

"Thanks. I have to admit, I'm feeling pretty good," I say.

Nothing can shake me today. Or at least that's what I was thinking.

"Why are you in such a good mood? Twelve answers are way more than you can keep in that little brain of yours. Say good-bye to the Wall of Fame Game, Mya Tibbs Fibs," says Naomi.

I put my backpack in my cabinet, and just as I'm about to spin around and let her have it, I get a picture of Mom rocking in Macey's room, and the little chair I used to sit in when I was two years old. Instead of blasting Naomi, I ask her a simple question.

"Why are you doing the Wall of Fame Game, Naomi?"

She rolls her eyes. "I told you before. If I can get on the wall, I'll be able to add that to my portfolio. Pageant judges and movie directors like that kind of stuff. Everything else, like our bet, is bonus points. And when I beat you, it will be sweet payback for what you did to me during Spirit Week."

Connie was right. Again. Beating me was not Naomi's main reason for making the wall. Why didn't I figure that out? Naomi should have never been my number one reason for making the wall.

I close my cabinet and say something I never dreamed I'd say to her.

"Good luck."

My classmates mumble and talk as I walk out of the cave. What they don't know is—Naomi's right. She figured things out long before I did. Her portfolio is important to her, not beating me.

In class, I swing my feet under my desk because I can't wait for my turn.

"Mya, you're up," says Mrs. Davis.

I've got a strut in my *ka-clunk*, and I don't care who sees it. Once Mrs. Davis closes the curtains and hits the egg timer, I switch gears because I'm ready!

"Here we go! Name four of the original thirteen American colonies."

I close my eyes and pretend I'm still listening to the tape. "Rhode Island, Connecticut, Massachusetts, and Georgie Porgie pudding and pie. Kissed the girls and made them cry."

My eyelids flip open. Did I say that out loud?

A huge wrinkle pops up in the middle of Mrs.

Davis's forehead. "What did you say?"

I swallow hard. "Georgia. The last original colony I said is Georgia."

My heart's bump-thumping again. I'm scared to close my eyes, but I definitely don't want to keep them open, either. Mrs. Davis shakes her head and reads the next question.

"Name the four stages of the water cycle."

My toes wiggle inside my boots as I answer. "Evaporation, condensation, precipitation, and collection."

"Good," she says.

My shoulders rise and come down slowly as I breathe out a bunch of air I didn't know I had in me. Whatever happened with my first answer must have been some weird brain mix-up. But now it seems to be over.

"Name four major organs in the human body."

I inhale and then exhale before I begin. "Okay, there's the lungs, the heart, the liver, and the wheels on the bus go round and round, round and round, round and round, the wheels on the bus go round and round, all day long."

Ding.

I stop singing and take a seat next to Mrs. Davis. If I'm lucky, this will be a bad dream, and my alarm clock will go off any moment now.

But it doesn't. This is really happening.

I feel the heat of Mrs. Davis's eyes staring at the side of my face. I can't look at her because I'm so embarrassed, and I don't even have an excuse for all the dumb things I just did.

Except . . .

"I was trying to say the brain as my fourth major human organ, but it was stuck behind the wheels on the bus and I couldn't say it. I know exactly what happened, Mrs. Davis. I listened to a recording while I slept last night, and it had some old nursery rhymes playing in the background. They must have stuck in my mind a lot better than the answers to the Wall of Fame Game questions."

"I see. That's very interesting." Then she drops the bad news. "Mya, you missed question number three. That's your first miss this week. One more incorrect answer, and you will be eliminated."

I feel her words. They sting, and I can't stop the tears from running down my face.

Mrs. Davis takes my hand. "Don't cry. You're not eliminated. You still have another shot. But tomorrow you have to answer every question correctly."

I stare at the floor, because I could be the next

person eliminated. "I know. Fifteen answers."

She nods. "That's right. But you can do it."

I lift my head to look at her. "I'm not so sure, Mrs. Davis. I know the questions are going to be harder tomorrow."

"But if you study, you'll get the job done." Mrs. Davis puts her arm around my shoulders and squeezes me close. I love her hugs, because I know she really cares about me.

"Listen to me, Mya Tibbs. Be confident. You can do this. But not making it isn't the end of the world. The only thing you'll lose is getting your name on the wall. Life will go on, okay?"

I nod, but it's not okay. It's not even true. If I don't make the Wall of Fame, everything will change. I'm just now understanding how important the Wall of Fame Game is for my little sister. And for me.

Usually Mrs. Davis is right. But today, she has no idea how wrong she is. I step out of the cave and, without looking at anyone, take my seat. I can feel the stares, but I refuse to look at anything except the top of my desk.

At recess, I tell Connie and the twins about the recording Nugget made for me, and how I was rappin' rhymes instead of answering questions.

"Did you get eliminated?" asks Connie.

"We're your friends, Mya, no matter what," says Starr.

"We're definitely your friends," adds Skye.

"I missed one," I say. "I'm one wrong answer away from wearing that lame T-shirt."

Connie puts her hands on her hips. "You listen to me, Mya Tibbs. We're going to make that Wall of Fame together, understand? You're not going to miss any more questions."

I nod.

Skye takes her sister's hand. Connie takes mine. The silence makes me feel worse.

"Don't miss another one, Mya," says Starr.

"No more misses," says Skye.

Starr takes my hand, and now all four of us walk like we're off to the see the wizard.

"We'll help you, right, Starr and Skye? That's what friends do," says Connie.

"You're very smart, Mya. We believe in you," says Starr.

"We definitely believe in you," says Skye.

"Thanks." I wish I believed in me. It's only going to get harder.

I'm so scared.

For the last few minutes, I've noticed Naomi

walking around me, not close, but enough for me to know she's there. She's like a vulture circling a wounded animal, waiting for it to die. How could she know that I missed a question?

She's eyeballing me, talking to two fifth-grade girls who wear expensive clothes and think they're better than everybody. Then she points at me, says something else, and all three girls laugh. She must know I missed one. But how?

Even though the twins make me smile, I'm still feeling nervous about everything going on in my life. I've got to get home and work harder than I've ever worked before. And after I study my Wall of Fame Game questions with Connie and the twins, I'll study Mom's recipe so I can figure out what she meant by not changing things.

The bell rings, and Mrs. Davis leads us back to class. My mind is so far from my schoolwork that by the time I stop daydreaming, Mrs. Davis is handing out Friday's Wall of Fame Game questions. I close my eyes, too scared to look. The questions get harder every day—so hard that I missed one today. I squeeze my eyes closed and pray. *Please, please don't be too hard.* Today, I wasn't ready for the Wall of Fame Game challenge. I'm nowhere close to being ready for the chili cook-off. I need Friday's questions to be a little easier.

I open my eyes, stare at the questions, and know my prayer didn't make it out of the classroom.

It's over.

WALL OF FAME GAME QUESTIONS FOR MYA TIBBS:

FRIDAY

1. Name five countries in Europe.

2. Name five national parks.

3. Name a populated or unpopulated Texas town for the first five letters of the alphabet without using Austin or Dallas.

Chapter Twenty-Five

At home, I drop my backpack on the couch and head toward Mom's room. That's when I see a note on the table.

Mya and Nugget,
I've taken your mom to the hospital. Macey
may arrive today! Will come get you if that
happens. Keep the phone close by.
Love, Dad

I check the back of the note for more information. Nothing. That's it? Jambalaya! Macey's coming!

She's not supposed to be here for another two weeks!

I dash down the hall to the nursery. The room smells like new furniture and baby lotion. There are gift boxes all over the floor, in the crib, on the dresser, and in the new car seat. I can tell Mom's been in here working, but it's far from being finished.

Macey's room was Mom's big project. If I didn't have these Wall of Fame Game questions to study, I'd help her. And even if I wasn't studying these questions, I've still got Mom's chili recipe to work on. Good gravy, I can't do everything! I'm only one person!

Wait a minute.

I pick up the phone, call Connie, and tell her my drama. "Can you bring your paints and markers, and anything else you can think of to decorate the room?"

"I need to study at least another hour, and then I'll come help. I'm surprised that I know almost all the answers to Friday's questions. What about you?" asks Connie.

"I'm in trouble. I know some of them, but not enough. And I can't miss another one like I did today."

"If I were you, I'd go back to what I knew was working. You didn't miss a question until you listened to that sleep CD Nugget made for you. Some things shouldn't be changed, Mya."

Mom said something about changing things, too. But I'll have to think about that later.

"Okay, Connie. Get here as soon as you can. I really need your help. Bye."

I call the twins, and even leave a message for Fish, then race upstairs and grab my study sheet that has all of the answers on it. I need to memorize fifteen answers before tomorrow, and there's no way I'm using Nugget's cell phone again.

I sit down at my computer desk and realize I may lose the chili cook-off. There's no way I can practice making chili today, with Mom in the hospital. And I think the most important thing is having Macey's room ready.

My chili wasn't that good anyway. It didn't taste anything like Mom's. On Sunday, I added too much garlic. Monday I supersized the veggies instead of making small veggies because it didn't take as much time. And then there was the whole issue about forgetting to put the meat in.

I think back to the times when Mom and I made chili. We would start on it right after I got my homework finished. She made snacks, and we'd talk about our day as we put the ingredients together. I'd hand them to her, and it seemed as if she took ten minutes stirring each vegetable into the chili pot. Mom and I stirred that chili all afternoon, and she was still stirring it when I went to bed.

We only made one practice pot, and it really wasn't practice. It was dinner for the next night! That's how good Mom and I were together. It took a lot of time, and patience, but . . .

Hold on.

That's what she was trying to tell me! Connie and I made chili twice this week, but we just threw stuff into the bowl and turned on the microwave. There was no letting the spices and vegetables and meat get to know each other. There was no slow stirring or talking to the chili. And there definitely wasn't any love. It didn't take us all evening. It took us ten minutes.

That's not enough time to make prize-winning chili. Mom knew, and tried to tell me when she quizzed me on the Wall of Fame Game questions. I hate that she's not here with me.

We've spent the whole week together going over questions and answers. She's cut up veggies and things for us to snack on while she quizzed me. If we had watched the Annie Oakley marathon, it would have just been Monday, Tuesday, and Wednesday. This was better.

Knock, knock!

I dash downstairs and peep through the side of the curtains. It's Connie, Nugget, and Fish! Perfect. I unlock the door.

"Hiya, Mya Papaya! I got a message that you need some help. Well, here I am, Super Fish Man to the rescue!"

I try to smile, even though I've got so many things on my mind. "Thanks, Fish. It's Macey's room. We have to hurry. Toys need to be put together and—"

"So what's the big rush?" asks Nugget.

I pull Nugget away from Connie and Fish and whisper what I know. "Dad left us a note on the table. Mom's in the hospital. That means Macey's coming. And I've got to study the Wall of Fame Game questions for tomorrow. I don't know how I'm going to get fifteen answers right."

Nugget's eyes widen. "Go study, Mya. I'll help Fish put the toys together."

Connie takes her art bag off her shoulder. "I got finished sooner than I thought. What do you want me to draw first?"

"Something that will help Macey feel safe at

night when she's alone," I say. "I'm going upstairs to unplug my laptop and bring it down here. That way I can work on my Wall of Fame Game questions and maybe help, too."

I go back to the kitchen table, knowing this last set of answers is going to make the difference in whether I get on the wall or not. Tonight may be the roughest night of studying for me, since I've got so many things on my mind. Mom's in the hospital, Macey's room isn't ready, I haven't practiced making chili in two days, and I've got fifteen answers to give tomorrow. It's going to take everything I've got to focus. I guess that's what For All My Efforts should mean.

The twins are coming up the sidewalk, so I *ka-clunk* to the door and let them in.

"Thanks for coming to help. I wish I had a better way of answering the Wall of Fame Game questions, but it looks like I'll be studying all night, and I don't even know where to start."

"You can do it, Mya," says Skye.

"You can definitely do it," says Starr.

They walk hand in hand behind me to Macey's room. I stop at the nursery door. My mouth drops open. "Whoa!"

Connie's drawn big beautiful clouds on the wall.

"That's amazing, Connie," I say.

"Thanks, but I'm nowhere close to being finished," she says. "How's the studying going?"

I shake my head. "Terrible. But I'm not giving up."

Nugget puts batteries in a train that chugs along the side of the crib. "Go study," he says.

Since the dining-room table is around the corner from the nursery, I can hear everything going on. When Connie asks about certain colors, I shout back.

"Make sure they're baby colors! Pink, blue, and yellow, colors like that."

When Fish asks if a lamp should go on her dresser or near the rocking chair, I yell to him.

"Put the lamp near the dresser!"

"Okay," he yells back.

The sound of laughter makes my concentration go away. "Keep it down! I can't study!"

"Sorry," yells Nugget, but I can still hear the giggles.

I put my hand on the computer mouse to click the browser button for the internet. But the arrow isn't moving. I move the mouse in circles, hoping it will snap out of its problem, but it doesn't. Then a little blue circle spins in the middle of the screen. It's just spinning and spinning. This is the worst time ever for the computer to freeze! I really wanted to look up a few things about national parks. I pull my braids to stop from screaming.

The laughter picks up again in Macey's room. I can't focus. Don't they understand how important this is? Don't they care that I need to study? I storm into the nursery.

"Hey, you guys! You are so . . ." My mouth shuts down. There's a tingle on my fingertips. My brain can't handle everything my eyes are trying to show it.

My friends stand proudly next to what they've made. They've got paint all over their faces, in their hair, on their clothes, on their fingers, but mostly, on the wall. And I can only think of one word to say.

"Jambalaya."

Chapter Twenty-Six

Right there on the wall in front of Macey's crib sits the entire Girl Galaxy Court: Animasia, Harmony, Queen Angelica, Jade-Iris, and Ice. They're the coolest warriors ever, and they were created by Connie. I've only seen them in one other place, and that's in Connie's special art room at school.

She wipes paint off her forehead. "It's the first thing I thought of that would make Macey feel safe."

In all the world, there cannot be a better best friend than the one I have. I give her a super-duper hug like the ones Mom gives to me. Fish taps my shoulder.

"Check out the shark in a baseball uniform with *Fish* written on the front. Now Macey will always know I'm around."

"That's awesome, Fish! Macey's going to love it," I say.

"May we have your attention, please?" asks Starr.

She and Skye are standing side by side, hiding something on the wall. Both smile the same smile as their heads move exactly at the same time to look at us.

Skye speaks first. "Everyone should have a twin. So we drew Macey's."

Starr moves to the left. Skye goes right, and a drawing of a little brown baby with sparkly eyes and lots of hair is on the wall.

Fish nods. "Boo-yang cool."

Nugget walks closer. "Is that baby glowing?"

"We brought glitter," says Skye.

"Lots of glitter," says Starr.

I'm stuck in stupid, staring at a brown glitter baby from outer space.

"You never told us you could draw," says Connie.

"You never asked," says Starr.

"Totally didn't ask," says Skye.

"What's her name?" asks Fish.

"Sears," says Starr.

"Macey's and Sears. Two perfect stores in the mall, right beside each other," says Skye.

Heads nod. It makes perfect sense.

"I love it, and so will Macey," I say. "But what was everybody laughing about?"

My brother speaks up. "Check it out, Mya." He points at the wall near him. There's a big, shiny nugget of gold with legs, feet, and a goofy face.

Fish cracks up laughing again. "It's so you. That's perfect, bro. Golden Nugget."

Nugget grins at me. "What do you think, Mya?"

I try to show a serious face, but I can't hold it. I point at the picture and giggle until it turns into belly-bustin' laughter. Everyone else laughs, too.

"Macey will have something to laugh at every day," I say.

"Think about all the taradiddles you can tell her using the pictures on her walls!" says Connie.

"Macey is going to love your taradiddles," says Starr.

"Absolutely love them," says Skye.

Fish steps closer to me. "And the good thing

about that is, she'll remember everything you tell her. Because your taradiddles always have some facts in them."

The smile slides from my face. Connie's, too. The twins stare at me. Fish scratches his head.

"Did I say something wrong?"

I shake my head. "You said something brilliant, Fish!"

"Good job, Fish," says Skye.

"Definitely a good job," says Starr.

"You'd better get to work, Mya," says Connie.

Fish lifts his hands in the air. "What? Would someone please tell me what I said that was so awesome?"

I giggle. "Sorry, you guys, but I have to go to my room and be alone. This is important. But before I go, I want to say thanks for helping me. Thanks for being the best friends ever."

Just as everyone leaves, Dad calls and says he and Mom will be home soon. He says something about false labor pains, and Macey isn't coming today. I hang up the telephone and give Nugget the news.

"I'm going to make me a couple of peanut-butter sandwiches and watch ESPN," says Nugget.

"Before you do that, would you please fix my

computer? It's frozen. I'll be in Macey's room if you need me,"I say.

In the nursery, I take a seat in the rocking chair. I lean forward, push the floor with the tips of my boots, and get a good rock going as I think about my family, my friends, and the Wall of Fame Game.

Just rocking, and smiling at the colorful walls, and seeing the awesome pictures that were made by my friends gives me goose bumps. I remember watching Mom sit and rock in this chair just yesterday. I bring my arms together like Mom had hers, when she was pretending that Macey was in her arms. I close my eyes, and it's easy to imagine that I'm rocking my baby sister. It feels so real that I begin to talk to her.

"If Mom doesn't like what my friends did to your wall, then I'll paint it. But did you know the Wall of Fame can never be painted over? It can't. Isn't that awesome? At first I didn't think it was a big deal. But now I do. I'm going to make that Wall of Fame, Macey."

I sit quietly and rock, as if I'm still holding her. As I move back and forth, my reasons for wanting to get on the wall move, too.

"I don't have to prove that cowgirls are smart. I need to prove to myself that I can do it. I need to show you that you can do it, too, Macey. One day, the names of our entire family will be on the Wall of Fame, and they'll stay there forever."

I stop rocking, walk to the crib, and pretend I'm putting my baby sister to bed. Very quietly, I pick up a crayon and draw a heart near her crib. Inside it, I write *Mya Loves Macey*, and then whisper, "I have to go study now. Talk to you later."

Chapter Twenty-Seven

Early Friday morning, I reach over and tap my alarm clock before it goes off. I've been wide awake for at least thirty minutes. Today's answers to my Wall of Fame Game questions circle my brain like an ambush.

But that's how I want it. And I'm going to wear my bright-orange church dress to school today. I want to look nice when Mrs. Davis tells me that I made the Wall of Fame.

Downstairs, Nugget and Dad wrestle on the floor for the newspaper. When I step into the room, they stop and look up, and I get straight to the point.

"Nugget, I'm leaving early again today, in case Connie needs some last-minute help with her Wall of Fame questions."

"Okay. I'm coming," he says.

"Good luck. You look very nice," says Dad.

I *ka-clunk* into Mom's room. She's sitting up, eating a bowl of fruit. "Don't you look spiffy! And you should. I'll be thinking about you, Mya. Do your best."

"Thanks, Mom! I will."

On the way to school, Nugget's talking nonstop, but I can't understand what he's saying, because I've got other things on my mind. I refuse to skip, kick rocks, sing, or talk to myself. I want to stay quiet, focused, ready for when it's my time in the cave with Mrs. Davis.

Nugget opens the school door for me, and I step inside. He grabs a strap of my backpack.

"You're going to make it, Mya. I'll be rooting for you. Let me know at lunch, okay?"

I nod and walk toward my classroom. "Thanks, Nugget. I'll let you know."

Everybody's in the cave, talking about who they think will make the Wall of Fame. Some of my classmates are helping others study. Naomi's at her cabinet. I try to ignore her, but she won't leave me alone.

"Where's that hat you had on earlier this week? You sure need it today! Definitely a bad hair day, don't you think? And an orange dress with a brown vest doesn't go with pink boots. I'm not only smarter than you are, I'm a better dresser, too! It doesn't matter. You're going to choke today, Mya. That Wall of Lame T-shirt is going to look even sillier with that outfit."

I ignore Naomi. Mrs. Davis walks in. "Good morning, students."

We all say good morning back as we put our things away. The twins come in and stand on both sides of me.

Starr grins. "Today's the big day."

"Definitely a big day," says Skye.

Connie puts her things away, and then comes over to where we're standing.

"Skye and Starr, can I talk to Mya alone for a minute?" she asks.

As soon as they walk away, Connie takes my hand and smiles. "Well, this is it, Mya. Today or no day. Are you ready?"

"Yes, I am. Are you?" I ask.

Connie chews her bottom lip. "I've never been this nervous. I'm so worried that I'm going to make two big mistakes when it's my turn. I can't get this far and then blow it, Mya. My stomach is full of butterflies."

I take her other hand. "We're going to do this together, Connie, as big sisters. You and me. For Clayton and Macey. For All My Efforts?"

Connie stops chewing her lip. She smiles, and I can tell she's calmed down.

"For All My Efforts," she says.

When the bell rings, we all wait for the intercom to crackle with static.

"Good morning, students. Let's stand for the Pledge of Allegiance."

I place my right hand over my heart, but I can feel Naomi's eyes on me from the left side of the room. I refuse to look at her. She doesn't matter anymore.

"This is your principal, Mr. Winky, yes, yes, yes! I hope you've had a wonderful week! There are just a few announcements this morning. First, we want to wish the remaining fourth graders still in the Wall of Fame Game a very special good luck! We also want to wish our first and second graders good luck as they hunt for signs of autumn on their field trip today. Also, several of our fifth graders are on the Bluebonnet Little League team. They open their season tomorrow, right after Bluebonnet's annual chili cook-off. Make plans with your family to attend. That will conclude this morning's announcements!"

Mrs. Davis writes in her attendance book as she calls our names. Moments later, Mrs. Hansen walks in. Mrs. Davis puts down her attendance book, picks up her clipboard, and smiles.

"Well, it's that time, class. For those of you still in the hunt to make the Wall of Fame, today is your last day of questions. I want to wish each of you good luck. When I call your name, please follow me into the cave. Lisa?"

Lisa's face wrinkles up. She lifts a tissue toward her face.

Ah . . . ah . . .

We all take cover, putting our heads down on our desks. The last thing I need right now is for Lisa McKinley to sneeze and blow my brains clean out of my head.

Ah . . . ah . . . achoooooooooooo!

"Bless you," I say.

She turns and smiles as she wipes her nose. "Thanks, Mya."

I'm thinking there was no sneeze damage until

I see Mrs. Hansen trying to rewrap her hair back into a bun.

When Lisa returns, she's almost running, smiling all the way to her desk. I'm so happy for her. Mrs. Davis is smiling, too.

"Mary Francis? It's your turn."

Mary talks to herself as she joins Mrs. Davis on their walk to the back of the cave. When she returns, I can tell she's been crying. Mrs. Davis looks sad, too. I know it's not right. I know it's mean. But I'm hoping Naomi Jackson looks just like that when she comes out of the cave.

Mrs. Davis lifts her clipboard. "Mya? It's your turn."

Wait a minute. She didn't call Naomi's name. That means . . .

Naomi missed two questions! She's disqualified!

I look over my shoulder at her. She's eyeballing me, thinking I'm going to say something smart and embarrass her. Instead, I get up from my seat and act like an older sister.

"I'm ready, Mrs. Davis."

I take my time *ka-clunk*ing down the aisle so Naomi can get a good look at my orange dress, brown vest, and pink boots that don't match. As we walk to the back of the cave, I take Mrs. Davis's hand. She smiles at me. "Glad to have you here on the last day, Mya."

"Glad to be here, Mrs. Davis."

She takes a seat and pulls the curtain. "Ready?"

"Yes, but I don't need you to ask me any questions, Mrs. Davis, because I know all the answers, and I'll give them in order. Sit back. Turn the egg timer on, because I'm going to tell you a little taradiddle."

Chapter Twenty-Eight

Mrs. Davis looks surprised, but she's grinning as she puts her copy of my questions on her lap. "There's no rule that says you can't tell a story for your answers. I'll listen for them, but you have to give me all the answers to question number one before you can give me answers to question number two and the same for question number three. Understand?"

"Yes, ma'am," I say.

"Good luck, Mya."

She taps the egg timer, and I start talking.

"I was on an early-morning trail with four of

my cowgirl friends. Their names all ended in A, just like mine. On this particular morning, I was so *Hungary* that I ate a *Belgium* waffle with *Turkey* bacon, fried in hot *Greece*. I asked our cook to hurry, but she said, 'Don't *Russia*,' so I didn't.

"After breakfast, we saddled up and headed toward the *Everglades*. We set up tents for a few days, fighting off a million acres' worth of alligators and swamp creatures before loading up and riding toward *Death Valley*. On our way, I found the prettiest *Yellowstone* near the *Grand Canyon* and shouted, 'This must be a *Rocky Mountain!*' But the other cowgirls with me weren't happy, because they missed being in Texas. So we turned around and went back home. I said good-bye to all my cowgirl friends whose names ended in A, just like mine. The only difference between me and them was, they were all named after Texas towns. *Alameda, Bandera, Clara, Dora,* and *Electra.* Happy trails, my friends, and long live the cowgirl nation!"

I don't need Mrs. Davis to tell me I did it.

Instead, I shuffle two steps to the right, tap my right heel twice with my left hand. Shuffle two steps to the left, tap my left heel two times with my right hand. Heel, toe, stomp. Heel, toe, stomp. Ride that horse, ride that horse! Turn and start again.

Mrs. Davis gets up and joins me! Yee-haw!

After the first turn, Mrs. Davis takes a seat. I sit next to her, and she looks over at me with a huge smile. "What was that dance we just did?"

"The Mya Shuffle," I say with a grin.

"You are amazing, Mya Tibbs. I can't believe what you just did! Congratulations, and welcome to the Wall of Fame."

I pump my fist. "Yippee-ki-yay!"

"Time to go back to class, Mya. I've still got a couple of your classmates to bring back here and give a chance to make the wall with you."

I tug at my vest, and the bottom of my dress, to make sure everything is where it's supposed to be. "Oh, yes, sure, okay."

I *ka-clunk* out of the cave like I'm famous. As I walk back into my classroom, I point at Connie and give her a thumbs-up. She stands and claps. "I knew you could do it! You rock, Mya Tibbs!"

"Okay, let's settle down," says Mrs. Davis.

I keep strutting toward my desk. That's right. I rock.

Mrs. Davis calls the next student. "Kenyan?"

As Kenyan passes my desk, he leans down and whispers. "Congratulations, Mya. I always knew you were smarter than Naomi."

"It's time to join your uncle on that wall," I say, pointing behind me with my thumb.

As Kenyan leaves with Mrs. Davis, and I sit at my desk, watching Mrs. Hansen's lips move but not really sure what she's saying because I'm too excited, I think about my family. Those who are here, and the one who isn't born yet, will be so proud of me.

Soon Kenyan comes out of the cave like Batman. He's racing to his seat with the biggest grin on his face. As he passes me, he leans down and whispers, "No more shame for Uncle Kenyan. I took care of it."

I nod and give him a fist bump. "Congratulations, Kenyan."

"Thanks, Mya."

Before I can stop smiling, Mrs. Davis calls a name that makes me nervous all over again.

"Connie?"

I turn around and watch her long legs take short steps up the aisle. She's looking around at everyone as she takes her hand and moves loose hair back behind her ear.

Soon, she follows Mrs. Davis into the cave, and the curtain closes. My knee bounces, and I'm not listening to Mrs. Hansen, because when that curtain opens, I want to be the first to see my best friend's face.

This is taking forever. What's going on? Suddenly the curtain opens, and my heart falls out of my chest and slams to the floor.

She's wiping her eyes, nodding her head, and walking toward me. I can't take it. I don't care if I get in trouble for being out of my seat. I *ka-clunk* over to her as fast as I can.

"It's okay, Connie. It's not the end of the world."

She sniffles. "I did it! We made the wall together!"

I cover my mouth because I don't know what else to do. It was one thing to talk about it, but now that we've done it, I feel like I'm going to explode with happiness. Something's squeezing my insides, and I just want to cut loose. If I could, I'd take Connie by the hand, run back into the cave, and have Mrs. Davis get up so the three of us could do the Mya Shuffle again!

Everything that's happened since Open House flashes through my mind. The reasons why making the wall was so important—her little brother, my little sister, my parents, everything.

"For All My Efforts," I say to her.

"For All My Efforts," she says back.

All through social studies and science, I hear Mrs. Davis talking, but my mind is still in the cave. I rewind my brain over and over again, answering question after question in the world's best taradiddle. I go back to Monday, Tuesday, Wednesday, even Thursday, when I missed one. It's the greatest movie I've ever seen. Right before lunch, Mrs. Davis makes the announcement that everyone's been waiting on.

"Class, it is with great pride that I read to you the names of this year's Wall of Fame Game winners. Please stand when I call your name. Lisa McKinley, Mya Tibbs, Kenyan Tayler, and Connie Tate. Let's give our winners a hand!"

I turn to Connie. Her face is still red from crying, but she smiles at me. I wave to my classmates and give thumbs-ups to the twins.

At lunch, Connie and I tell Nugget and Fish that we made the wall.

Fish gives us high fives. "That's awesome! Congratulations!"

Nugget fist-bumps us and then holds up his milk as if making a toast. All the fifth-grade boys at the table raise their milk cartons as my brother speaks.

"Breaking news! My sister and her best friend, Connie, made the wall. Hooray!"

"Hooray!"

Solo Grubb struts toward my brother's table with his sunglasses on and completely changes the mood.

"Yo, Nugget, what you're teaching the team about pitches is going to change everything."

I don't want to talk about baseball, but Nugget nods at Solo as he struts by and then grins at us. "You should come over to the ballpark today for a quick minute. I want you to hear something."

"Maybe for a minute, but you know I've got chili to make."

"Cool. You should come, too, Connie," says Nugget.

She smiles and pushes loose hair behind her ear. She keeps staring at my brother. He's staring back at her. And they're both smiling a little longer than they should. I get uncomfortable, so I take Connie's arm and drag her to our table near the stage. I refuse to talk about the way she's looking at my brother, and the way he was looking back at her. Instead, we eat and talk, and laugh, just like best friends are supposed to after a day like this.

"I'll be a few minutes late to recess," says Connie. "I've got to go get something out of my art room."

She's grinning at me, and I know exactly what she's going to get. Naomi's not going to be happy, but right now, I'm the happiest girl on the planet!

At recess, someone's playing music, and as soon as Connie comes back, she starts dancing the Mya Shuffle. "Come on, Mya! Let's teach the twins how to do it!"

Soon the four of us are dancing, and others join in. Lisa and Kenyan show up.

"Are you ready?" asks Lisa.

"For what?" I ask.

"The walk," says Kenyan.

"Jambalaya! I forgot all about that! Come on, Connie," I say.

We all walk side by side, not in a line, but straight across, taking up lots of room on the playground. Boys and girls move out of our way and give us all the space we want. Fourth and fifth graders point as we walk by. I know what they're saying.

"They made the Wall of Fame."

For the first time, Naomi stays as far away from me as she can. I almost feel sorry for her. That T-shirt with all the flowerhead babies on it is going to ruin her reputation. She may never win another beauty pageant!

But it was her bet, not mine.

That'll teach her to never mess with a member of the cowgirl nation!

Chapter Twenty-Nine

Once we're back in class, it seems as if the clock has slowed down. When the bell finally rings, everybody dashes to the cave. There's whispering and giggling, but when I walk in, my classmates clap. Naomi's standing alone by her cabinet. Her face is covered with mad, and I'm wondering if she's going to back out.

Connie reaches inside her cabinet, removes the black plastic bag, pulls out the lame T-shirt, and hands it to Naomi. "You lost the bet. Don't you have something to say to Mya?"

She bows the shortest bow in the history of bows

and then rolls her eyes at me. "This week, you were smarter than me, Mya Tibbs Fibs. But that doesn't mean you'll be smarter than me forever and eternity."

Naomi takes the shirt from Connie, pulls it over her head, and then sticks her arms through the sleeves. Everyone is giggling.

Naomi closes her cabinet door, and we all move as she makes her way toward our classroom. Even Mrs. Davis stares at Naomi as she walks by her desk. We all follow her out into the hall, waiting to see the reaction from the rest of the kids in our school.

Three fifth-grade girls walk down the hall and stop. "Naomi? What the what?"

She rolls her eyes. "Fashion trend. Wear what others won't, and make it look good."

One girl touches the shirt. "That is so fab. I want one!"

The other girls agree and walk with Naomi down the hall.

"Unbelievable," says Connie.

"That would never happen to me," I say.

I still feel like gold. I kept my promise to Macey. And in nine years, it will be her turn.

After school, I'm not sure if my boots are touching the sidewalk on my way to the ballpark. It's as if I'm floating down the street with Connie, Nugget, and Fish. Kids from school pass us and wave.

Minutes later, we're at the ballpark. Nugget and Fish dash to the restroom and soon come out in baseball clothes. Two of Nugget's teammates jog over to him.

"We practiced what you taught us last night. And we watched that YouTube video on pitching. We're killing the ball, bro. Watch."

His teammates take turns hitting the ball. Nugget and the coach clap. Suddenly my brother whistles. "Hey, everybody gather around. I've got an announcement to make."

Nugget stands near Connie and me. I'm so excited to hear what he has to say that I don't see Dad come in.

"What's going on?" he asks.

"Nugget's going to make an announcement," I say.

Once the team gathers, my brother moves to the middle of the huddle. "I've been trying to figure out how I can be a better team player. And I think I've figured it out. I quit."

It's another bad surprise. I can't breathe.

"What are you, crazy? We need you," says Solo.

Before Coach can say anything, Nugget continues. "I'd like to quit as a player and rejoin as an assistant coach. Here's why. I can't explain why I keep striking out, or why I can't catch the ball very well in the outfield. But I don't think there's anybody out here who knows more about baseball than I do."

"You sure taught me how to hit that curveball. That was boo-yang," says Solo.

Another teammate talks. "I couldn't hit a slider. Now I can, thanks to you."

Fish steps up. "I didn't realize a knuckleball doesn't spin until Nugget showed me what it looks like leaving a pitcher's hand. Now when I see it coming, I'm ready to hit it out of the park!"

Coach blows his whistle, takes off his hat, and scratches his head. "Micah . . . I mean, Nugget, if you would like to take on the role of my assistant coach, I think it would be an honor to this team."

Dad leaves Connie and me, hops the fence, and pulls Nugget to him. Nugget hugs him back as tears drip from Dad's chin.

"You make me so proud."

"I figured out how I can help my team, Dad."

The team claps, pulls Nugget away from Dad, and raises him on top of their shoulders. They carry him all the way back to the dugout. I can't help but grin.

Soon Dad leaves, and Connie and I head home. Before she turns down her street, she looks at me. "Are you going to work on the chili today? I can help."

I shake my head. "But would you draw a really big picture to hang on my booth tomorrow? That might help. I'll be there early, at seven o'clock. Last night I figured out what Mom has been trying to tell me all week about changing things. I just hope I didn't learn that lesson too late."

"I'll make that picture for you tonight," she says. "See you tomorrow morning. I'm glad Nugget figured out a way to help his team. I guess you don't always have to be one of the players."

Wait a minute.

I wave to Connie as she walks toward her apartment building. An idea has popped into my head, and I think it's a good one. All week I've been making chili the wrong way. I've rushed it, cut the veggies too big, didn't pay attention, forgot to add things. I might not get it right. But there is something that I'm really good at doing, and tomorrow, at the cook-off, I'm going to do it!

This is my last chance to get it right. It's now or never.

As soon as I get home, I head to the kitchen,

wash my hands, and set my mind on making the best chili ever. I chop my vegetables into tiny little pieces. I stir them all together in a bowl, pretending it's a skillet, nice and gently. As I pour in my tomato sauces and spices, I talk to them, and let them know I need them to make friends with the vegetables in the bowl. I even breathe through my nose so I can smell everything forming a nice little family.

After I add a package of the pre-cooked meat Dad bought for me, I stir everything one more time, then put it all in the microwave for ten minutes. When the microwave dings, I stir my bowl of chili, and put it back in for five more minutes.

It smells so good.

When I turn around to go sit at the table, Mom's standing there, smiling at me.

"I can tell by the aroma that this one is going to be your best batch."

"Thanks, Mom. I'm really focused on making good chili the way you make it. But at the cook-off tomorrow, I'm going to add something that I'm good at doing. And I'm going to do it Annie Oakley style!"

Chapter Thirty

It was an awesome surprise, not a bad one, to see Mom up and dressed this morning. Usually she's still in her robe and slippers. But today she's wearing her Annie Oakley outfit! And I'm wearing mine! Holy moly!

"How many braids do you want today, Mya?" she asks.

I take off my cowgirl hat and sit in the chair. "Five. One for every person in my family," I say.

As she's fixing my hair, Mom tells me something I don't expect.

"I'm going with you to the chili cook-off. Your

dad is bringing me a special chair and pillows so I can keep my legs up. I can't help, but I can be there. I'm so proud of you, Mya. Even though it's supposed to be ninety degrees today, I wouldn't miss this for anything."

I want to say something, but I can't. For a whole week I figured Mom didn't want to do anything with me now that Macey was coming.

That wasn't true. I was wrong.

Mom quizzed me just about every day to help with the Wall of Fame Game questions. She told me how happy she was that Macey had me for a big sister. And best of all, she let me know that she was happy that I was her first daughter. And she wouldn't want it any other way.

Finally, I know exactly what I need to tell her.

"I love you, Mom."

"I love you, too, Mya."

As soon as Dad comes into the kitchen, I hand him a sheet of paper.

"What's this?" he asks.

"I need those things for the cook-off. And I have to have them before the judges come to my booth, okay? Will you bring them to me?"

He winks and then starts tickling me. It's the perfect morning, and if Dad comes through with my supplies, I've got a good shot at winning another apron for Mom.

Dad drops us off near the baseball fields. There are fifteen chili booths set up, and one booth that has "Judges Only" written across the top of it. It's empty, but I'm sure the judges will be here soon. Some of the competitors are already here, and I can smell onions, bell peppers, garlic, and chili powder cooking in skillets.

I spot Mrs. Frazier. She eyeballs me and throws up a wimpy wave. I wimpy-wave back.

Just seeing her makes me think about what she did at Dad's store. I want her to know that the best she's going to do today is second place.

Instead I ignore her, the same way I did Naomi, and find my booth. It's the last one. That's where the champion from the year before has to be.

It takes Dad awhile to set up my stove, which is one we use for camping. I can tell he's cleaned it up because it's so shiny, it looks almost new! There are two burners on the stove, and a short counter where I can chop my vegetables.

I've never cooked on a stove before. I'm so nervous that I'm going to burn something. I only get one shot, and I know it has to be right.

After he gets Mom's chair and pillows out of the

car and helps her to my booth, Dad lights my burners for me and turns them down low.

"I'm going back to the house. Your brother and I will be back before the judges get started." He kisses my forehead. "Good luck. You're going to do great."

"Thanks, Dad," I say. "Don't forget that list of things I gave to you this morning."

Dad's head tilts to one side. "Sure, but why do you need Buttercup?"

"It's a surprise. Please bring him, okay?"

He shrugs. "Okay, I'll bring him. See you later."

Mrs. Frazier walks by our booth. Mom smiles and waves.

"Good morning, Mrs. Frazier! Good luck!"

"Mom," I say. "She wants to take our title away! Why would you wish her good luck?"

I sit on the arm of Mom's chair and shoot eyeball bullets at Mrs. Frazier as she walks by. Mom takes my hand.

"When I first entered this contest five years ago, I did it because I loved to cook, and I wanted to win. Then you became old enough to help me. Everything changed. Making chili in the kitchen with you for the cook-off became one of my most favorite things to do. I didn't start winning until you and I did it together. We're a good team, Mya. I don't care about winning. I just enjoy the time I spend with you. That's the only reason I'm out here today."

She reaches inside a bag and pulls out two thermoses. "I remembered your hot chocolate and my coffee. We always have this before we start cooking."

I take my thermos, lean over, and put my head on Mom's shoulder. She's never told me this story. Making chili was never about winning. It was always about us.

When Mrs. Frazier walks by again, I smile at her, because I have a better reason for making chili than just beating her.

But I'm still going to win.

The first thing I grab is my skillet. I'm going to fry my chili meat slowly and add the spices to it while it cooks. Mom encourages me as I measure out the spices and sprinkle them on top of the meat as it cooks.

"Take your time, Mya," she says.

I reach inside another bag and take out an onion and the special Kitchen Kids vegetable chopper Mom lets me use. I set them both on the counter and chop those onions into tiny pieces. When I'm finished, I grab a bowl from a bag and put the onions in it.

"Very good," says Mom.

I do the same for the bell peppers and the tomatoes. When I'm finished, I sprinkle the vegetables in with the meat and stir it again. It smells so good. I sit on the edge of Mom's chair and talk to her as I watch my chili cook slowly.

Other competitors show up, and soon all fifteen booths are filled with people. Someone claps, and I look up to see two men and one lady walk into the "Judges Only" booth. They wave at everyone. I wave back and try to stay calm, but my heart thumps like I'm watching a scary movie. The sun rises higher in the sky, and I'm getting itchy and sweaty in my Annie Oakley outfit, but I can't let the heat distract me. I stir my chili and stay focused.

The air smells like food, and people gather around to watch. I can tell by the wonderful smell coming from my pot that the meat and all of the ingredients have become family and will soon be one big pot of love.

"Hey, Mya!" Connie comes by with a big rolled-up paper. "I think you're going to like this."

When she unrolls it, I clap my hands and hug her. "It's awesome! Tape it to the side of my booth!"

Connie frowns. "But then some people won't be able to see you cooking."

I don't care. Connie's picture of a wagon trail with cowboys and cowgirls eating chili while sitting on rocks and tree stumps is perfect! Even Mom's impressed.

As Connie tapes the picture to the front of my booth, people stop and talk about it. I can hear their conversations about chili and the Wild West as I get ready for the judges. Even the twins stop by, dressed in matching blue jeans, cowboy hats, and red western blouses.

Skye waves. "Howdy, Mya! Look what we're wearing! We came to watch you win!"

Starr tucks her thumbs in the loops of her jeans. "You're definitely going to win, Mya."

A microphone blares across the area. "The judges are about to begin tasting chili in search of this year's winner! Good luck to all you fine chili makers!"

Where's Dad? He's late! I need Buttercup, or my plan is going to flop.

I take the top off my pot of chili and stir it slowly. That's what Mom would do to calm down. I listen as people clap at other booths. The judges are taking forever to come down the line. They're talking to people and laughing. I'm nervous, but stirring the chili calms me.

It's not long before the judges are at the booth right before mine. They sound very nice, and they're telling the people next to me that their chili is very, very good. My heart sinks. Maybe I should stir mine again. I hope Dad gets here soon.

Those three judges seem to be spending a lot of time with my booth neighbor. I keep stirring, hoping my chili gets better with each stir. Moments later, the three judges step inside my booth. One man wears a bow tie, the other has a straight tie. I'm feeling pretty good because the lady is dressed like a cowgirl. She smiles at Mom.

"Congratulations, Monica. I haven't had a chance to get by your house to see you. Are you having a boy or a girl?"

"It's a girl," says Mom.

Thump!

I step outside my booth to see what made that noise. It's Fish and Nugget, rolling Buttercup toward my booth. Dad and Mr. Leatherwood are carrying the tree stumps.

"I made it," says Dad.

I hug him. "Thank you! This helps me so much!"

The guys set the stumps right in front of my booth.

The lady judge leans down to talk with me. "We're ready to taste what you've got in that pot!"

"Yes, ma'am. I'm ready now," I say.

Chapter Thirty-One

I reach inside a bag and grab three bowls, fill them halfway with chili, and give one to each judge. "Please take a seat on a stump, and I hope you enjoy my presentation."

Their eyebrows rise as each one takes a seat.

"Dad, will you put me on Buttercup?"

"Sure thing," he says.

Once I'm sitting on Buttercup, I pull a paper from my vest pocket and tell a Texas-sized tara-diddle.

"This whole week, I've been learning facts about things that I would never have known had I not signed up for the Wall of Fame Game. And the things I learned got me thinking about this chili cook-off. How many people really know where chili came from?"

People gather closer to my booth. I see the head of one lady moving closer until she works her way to the front. It's Mrs. Davis. She grins at me, and I grin back before continuing.

"Today is your lucky day. I looked up chili on the internet and found out a few things. I think some are taradiddles, but you can believe what you want. Here's what I found out."

I signal Dad over. "Would you please turn Buttercup to level one?"

"Sure thing," he says.

Buttercup slowly moves as I hold on with one hand and hold my paper with the other. "A long time ago, like long before I was born, there was a Spanish nun who believed she had out-of-body experiences that would totally fly her spirit across the Atlantic to preach Christianity to the Native Americans. Once on her way back home, her spirit wrote down the recipe for chili, and said to make it with green peppers, venison, onions, and tomatoes."

There's a few giggles in the crowd, but I keep talking.

"And then there were these people from the Canary Islands. Oh, this was also a long time ago, before I was born. They moved to San Antonio and made some chili. They used local peppers, wild onions, and various meats. But this dude named J. C. Cooper, who lived near Houston, said something like this: 'When the poor families of San Antonio have to buy their meat in the market, a very little is made to suffice for the family; it is generally cut into a kind of hash with nearly as many peppers as there are pieces of meat—this is all stewed together.'"

I fold my paper, stuff it back in my vest, and smile at the crowd. "I believe Mr. Cooper."

And then I open my mouth and sing like I'm in concert. Dad changed the words to "She'll be Comin' Round the Mountain When She Comes" into a song about me. I added a verse to make it special for the chili cook-off.

"She'll be making bowls of chili when she comes.
They'll be lickin' all their fingers and their
thumbs!
Even though she's a beginner, Mya's chili is a
winner!
She'll be making bowls of chili when she
comes!"

As long as the judges eat, I sing. I watch their feet tap the ground as I belt out my song. People clap their hands. The twins lock arms and do-si-do, and then grab people in the audience and swing them around, too! It's a party at my booth!

Once the judges finish, they hand me their bowls.

"I've never seen such a wonderful chili cook-off performance in the ten years I've been judging," says the man in the bow tie.

"What a fabulous job you did, young lady," says the judge in the straight tie.

The lady winks at me. "That was some mighty fine singing, and I took a real liking to Buttercup," she says.

"Thank you," I say to each judge before they leave.

They shake my hand, shake Mom's hand, and the lady judge tips her hat at me. I tip mine back. Soon, the three of them are back in their "Judges Only" booth and huddle together. Cook-off competitors step out of their booths and talk to each other. I stand outside my booth, too, because I know the judges loved what I did.

Suddenly, a microphone squeaks, and all talking stops.

"And now it's time to announce the winner," says the judge in the bow tie. The lady judge takes the microphone and walks to a spot in front of all the booths.

"This has been one of the best chili cook-offs in Bluebonnet's history! We've had everything from sweet chili, to spicy, and even a history lesson on chili with a boot-tapping show! Unfortunately, we can only choose one winner. This year's chili cook-off winner is Mr. Bob Johnson, in booth number four!"

The smile crumbles off my face.

I can't bear to look at Mom. I let her down. I let the family down. All this extra stuff for nothing. I had Dad bring Buttercup and all these stumps. . . .

I slowly *ka-clunk* over to Mom, trying not to cry, but I can't help it. I sit on the edge of her chair and lean on her shoulder. She leans her head on mine, and we're just quiet for a moment. There's a line of people, waiting to shake my hand.

"Good job, little girl. That was awesome."

"Thanks," I say.

Another lady steps up. "Nice job. You were the highlight of the cook-off."

I nod and shake her hand. Mom reaches for me. I put my arms around her neck, and she gives me a super-duper hug and then whispers, "They're right. You did a great job, Mya."

"But I didn't win, even though I followed your recipe. I'm sorry."

The lady judge steps into our booth. "Little lady, I'm getting ready to leave, but I wanted to tell you that you did a fine job today, and I really enjoyed myself at your booth. I'll be looking for you again next year."

I wipe the tears from my face. "But why didn't I win?"

The lady judge grabs a spoon, dips it into my pot, and eats another mouthful.

"Your chili is excellent! I'd know it if I was blindfolded. It tastes just like last year's winner. But there were lots of good chili recipes this year. Y'all have fun today!"

As she leaves, I think about what she said, and a grin spreads across my face. When I turn to Mom, she's already grinning.

"That's right, Mya. Your chili tastes exactly like mine from last year! You did it!"

I wrap my arms around her again, but this time it's not because I'm sad. Now I know what she meant when she said it wasn't about winning. "You were right, Mom. Making prize-winning chili has nothing to do with a prize. I had so much fun. How about we cook together every day? You can teach me all your recipes, and I promise I won't rush them."

Mom smiles and rubs her belly. Dad comes over and gives me a fist bump. I'm okay with it, because I've already gotten my super-duper hug from Mom. He points to the baseball field.

"The game's starting. Mya, you gather up all of the utensils and spices. Leave Buttercup and the tree stumps for me and your brother. I'm going to the field to be with Nugget, okay?"

"Sure, Dad. We'll be fine," I say.

Dad jogs across the grass to the ballpark. Connie and the twins help me take my bags and utensils to the truck. I tell my friends what the judge said about the chili.

"It was good. She liked it," I say. "She even said it tasted like Mom's winning chili from last year. She remembered it."

"Excuse me . . . Mya?"

I turn around. It's Mrs. Frazier. Oh, no. The twins freeze. So does Connie.

"I don't want to keep you long, but I just wanted to say you did a fine job today. I didn't know the history of chili, and I thought your song was so much fun. I'll be trying again next year, and I hope you do, too. See you in church tomorrow."

"Thanks, Mrs. Frazier," I say.

"Something happened to her," says Skye.

"Something definitely happened to her," says Starr.

"Maybe her chili was bad," says Skye.

"Green chili-itis comes from bad chili," says Starr.

Just as I set a bag down in the back of Dad's truck, I hear my name again.

"Mya!"

It's Mom! I rush to her side. Connie and the twins run with me.

"What's wrong? Are you okay?"

"My water just broke."

Skye shakes her head. "Water doesn't break."

"It's a liquid," says Starr.

Connie pushes me. "Go get your dad and your brother! Macey's downloading!"

Chapter Thirty-Two

At the hospital, two nurses come to the car and put Mom in a wheelchair. Dad walks with her. "Mya, Nugget, go to the labor and delivery waiting room on the fourth floor. I'll meet you there as soon as I can."

"Okay, Dad," I say.

Nugget's in his baseball uniform. I'm in my cooking apron. Dad's wherever Mom is. My brother and I pace the floor in the labor and delivery waiting room at Bluebonnet General Hospital.

"I didn't even get to coach my first game," says Nugget. "But this is more important."

I nod. "Duh."

There's lots of people in here. Some are reading books. Others watch television. Some are asleep in their chairs, while others eat as they wait for news.

After an hour, I can't pace anymore. I take a seat, and Nugget sits next to me. Dad hasn't come to talk to us. I hope Mom and Macey are okay.

And then the waiting room door opens.

Dad appears in a blue gown with a little blue hat on his head. His smile is wider than the Pacific Ocean.

"She's here. Come meet your little sister."

Dad takes our hands and leads us down the hall. I begin to skip. Then I walk again. I can't figure out how I want to get to Macey, but I want to get there fast.

"Your mom is doing great. She'll be ready for you to visit her very soon."

We walk through two big doors, and then farther down that hall. Soon we're standing in front of a huge window. Dad points to a tiny white crib with a pink sign on it that says *Baby Macey Tibbs, 6 Pounds, 5 Ounces.* I press my face to the glass. Nugget does, too.

There she is, with lots of black curls on her head. Her mouth opens, and she yawns so big that she startles herself. I giggle. She's beautiful.

I watch Macey squirm around under her blanket. She's so tiny and perfect. A nurse appears at the window, points at us, and then at Macey. Dad looks my way.

"The nurse wants to know if you want to hold your little sister."

Nugget backs away from the window. "No, not yet. I might break her."

I step in front of my brother. She doesn't need to meet him first. She needs me. I'm the big sister, the one who's going to answer her questions, help her when she needs it, care about her folder full of A+ papers, and be the example she'll need for the rest of her life.

"I'm ready to hold her," I say.

After washing my hands two times, and putting on a gown and hat like Dad's, I sit in a chair, and the nurse shows me how to make a cradle with my arms. And when I do, they place Macey's little body in it, all wrapped up in a blanket. She's asleep, so I hold her closer, hoping she can hear my heartbeat. I could hold her like this all day and all night, because she weighs less than my backpack!

Then her eyes open, and she looks right at me.

Her ears are so tiny, I don't want to hurt them

when I talk. So, as softly as I can, I speak to her for the first time. "Hi, Macey. I'm Mya, your big sister."

She keeps staring at me, like she already knows. And at that very moment, I'm so happy that I took the Wall of Fame Game challenge.

The nurses let me hold her for ten more minutes before putting her back in her little white crib. As I take off the gown and hat, I already miss her.

"We'll bring her to your mom's room soon," says the nurse.

Dad and Nugget are gone when I come out of the nursery, so the nurse walks me to Mom's room. Mom is smiling, even though she looks like she doesn't feel very good.

"I'm just a little sore, but I'll be fine tomorrow," she says.

I'm telling Mom, Dad, and Nugget about what it felt like to hold Macey when Fish and his dad walk in. Fish's baseball uniform is dirty from the shirt to his shoes. But he walks up to me with a huge smile and talks in a whisper.

"Hiya, Mya Papaya! I just saw Macey. She looks just like you!"

I stop smiling, because Macey's head was shaped more like Nugget's. And her skin was peeling. But I bet Fish meant that in a nice way. So I smile again.

He hands Nugget a baseball. "We won, bro, eight to nothin'. The team wants you to have the game ball. We couldn't have done it if you hadn't shown us how to see pitches."

My brother takes the ball from Fish. His teammates' signatures are all over it. Dad puts his arm around Nugget.

"Nothing like getting the game ball, son," he says.

Mr. Leatherwood steps forward and shakes Dad's hand. "Good-lookin' baby you got there, Tibbs. Congratulations."

"Thank you," says Dad.

"We're celebrating the win at the Burger Bar tomorrow at noon. Think you and Nugget might make it?"

Dad nods. "We'll be there."

Nugget's still looking at his baseball, but I can see a grin bigger than the baseball field on his face. Soon Connie, her parents, and the twins and their parents come in. While the grown-ups talk to Mom and Dad, Fish, Nugget, Connie, the twins, and I go back to the nursery.

The nurse sees us and moves Macey to the front so we can have a better look.

Connie puts her arm around me. "You're finally a big sister," she says.

"Yep! And I got to hold her already."

"She looks just like Sears," says Skye.

"Just like Sears," says Starr.

Holy moly.

I think back to the picture the twins painted on Macey's wall. They're right. Macey looks just like Sears! How did they do that? I've always thought the twins could be from another planet. There's so much proof, and the picture of Sears on the wall just adds to the list. But they're my friends, and whether or not they're aliens doesn't matter.

"I've got good news," says Connie. "My parents are throwing me a party next Saturday to celebrate me making the Wall of Fame, and you're all invited!"

I give my best friend a hug. She's getting what she wanted, and she deserves it. Making that Wall of Fame was hard work.

One by one, everybody leaves. Dad and Nugget sit on the little couch near Mom's bed. I'm sitting on her bed, holding her hand, smiling at her.

Knock. Knock.

"It's just me and a really cute baby named Macey," says the nurse as she rolls the little white crib next to Mom's bed. Nugget leans in and takes a closer look.

"She's beautiful, Mom."

Dad kisses my forehead. "I think she looks like you, Mya."

I glance at Nugget. He rolls his eyes, and I giggle. Mom's eyelids open and close very slowly. Dad steps over and kisses her forehead, too. "I'm going to take Nugget and Mya home. You and Macey get some sleep. You both have had a long day. We'll be back in the morning. Call or text if you need me to bring you anything, okay? I love you."

Mom nods as her eyelids close and don't open again. Dad puts a finger to his mouth for us to be quiet as we leave. I take one last look at Macey and whisper, "I'll be back tomorrow."

"Me, too," says Nugget.

On our way home, Dad stops at Dairy Queen. It's the perfect ending to a perfect day, knowing Mom and Macey are fine. It feels even better knowing that soon our whole family will be together.

But I can't help but wonder . . . is Mom going to be too busy with Macey to do anything else with me? What if the chili cook-off was the last thing we'll get to do together?

Chapter Thirty-Three

Sunday morning, instead of going to church, Dad, Nugget, and I head to the hospital. My brother's wearing another one of his goofy T-shirts. This one reads *Dear Mr. Algebra, Solve Your Own Problems. I Got Enough of My Own.*

Macey's in the room with Mom, but she's asleep. We wash our hands and then take turns holding her. She's so little, wrapped in that baby blanket.

Mom tells us that she's not feeling nearly as sore today as she was yesterday, and that she and Macey will get to come home tomorrow.

Nugget gets to hold Macey first and keeps asking,

"Is she okay? Am I holding her right?"

I glance at the clock. Nugget's held her for ten minutes. That's long enough.

"It's my turn," I say, and cross my arms to make a bowl for Dad to sit her in. He takes Macey from Nugget and gives her to me. I feel like a professional baby holder.

Dad is the last one to hold Macey. I even like watching him hold her. Nugget sits close to him, and they talk about her little hands, and whether or not she'd be able to throw a curveball.

Thirty minutes later, Dad puts Macey in Mom's arms.

"We'll be back in a couple of hours," says Dad as he and Nugget head toward the door.

Mom and I wave as they leave. "Congratulations again, Nugget," I say.

He nods and smiles as he holds up a baseball. "Game ball, baby."

Dad nudges my brother. "Gee, Nugget, your head is getting awfully big. Will it fit through the door?"

Mom and I laugh as they push on each other until we can't see them anymore. Mom points to the nightstand.

"Mya, will you reach in the first drawer and pull out that bag for me?"

I do, and hand the sack to Mom. She presses her call button for the nurse. I stand and rush to her bed.

"Is everything okay? You're not in pain, are you? Is there something I can do? What's wrong?" I ask.

When the nurse comes in, she's smiling. "Are you ready?" the nurse says.

Mom pulls a video case out of the bag. "We're ready! Pop this in for us, will you please?"

She hands a DVD to the nurse and then gives me the case. I look at the movie title and almost fall out of my seat. *Annie Oakley: The Complete Series*! I flip it over and read the back out loud.

"Mom, there's thirty-six hours of Annie Oakley's television shows on these DVDs!"

She giggles. "That's right. I imagine one hour a day for a whole month should take care of our Annie Oakley cravings. And Macey needs to catch up. Now get over here and climb in the bed with us so we can watch a couple hours before the guys come back."

"Too bad Buttercup's not here," I say as I take my boots off and climb in next to her. I lay my head on Mom's shoulder and give Macey my pinkie finger. She grabs it and squeezes, just as the show comes on.

Mom lets out a mouthful of air. "It's never too early to train a new cowgirl. Right, Mya?"

I giggle and kiss my sister on the forehead. "It's never too early."

Acknowledgments

I'd like to thank God for the gift of writing. I believe He had his cowboy boots on when He helped me with this one! I'm having so much fun writing about Mya, her family, and her friends, but I have family and friends of my own who deserve a "Yee-haw," and I'd like to give it to them.

First, a big Texas shout-out to my incredible husband, Reggie, and those two amazing sons of mine, Phillip and Joshua. You are truly a blessing in my life. Also, I'd like to send a very special thank-you to my brother-in-law, Darrell Ray, for taking care of things for me so that I could write without being disturbed.

Thank you, Kay Reidy, fourth-grade teacher at West Elementary School in Independence, Iowa, for sharing information about your classroom online. Your amazing website gave me several ideas, which led me to the Mastery Club!

Thank you, Heather Renz, for creating the Mastery Club and giving me permission to use it in *The*

Wall of Fame Game. Anyone wishing to purchase the Mastery Club, or view the many teaching tools created by Mrs. Renz, should visit her website at http://www.mrsrenz.net/forstudents/masteryclub-mc.htm.

Thank you, Juliet White, Tim Kane, Varsha Bajaj, and Laura Ruthvan for helping me stay focused on all of Mya's drama! She made it through, and I have your thoughtful critiques to thank for that.

Thank you, Dixie Keyes, for your friendship and for reading *The Wall of Fame Game* when you came to visit me for vacation. I put you to work and you never complained. What a true friend.

I'm so thankful for all of my family members and mentors who encourage me, especially Barbara Scott, Christine Taylor-Butler, Donna Gephart, and Neal Shusterman.

Alessandra Balzer and Donna Bray, you proved to me how vested you are, not only in my writing but in me. Caring is clearly a huge part of who you are, and I'm so grateful to be a part of your team.

Kristin Rens, your comments, questions, and ideas helped me take *The Wall of Fame Game* to a level I would have never reached without you. And you did it with encouragement, kindness, and friendship. You are amazing. Working with you makes me want to write, and I hope you continue to be my editor until we both choose to put our pens down.

Jen Rofé, the longer we're together, the more I love you. Sometimes I forget you're my agent, because our relationship is more like family. Thank you for being that person in my life.

—Crystal